Sophomores

Published by Merlyn's Pen, Inc.
4 King Street
P.O. Box 1058
East Greenwich, Rhode Island 02818-0964

Printed in the United States of America.

These are works of fiction. All characters and events portrayed in this book are fictional, and any resemblance to real people or incidents is purely coincidental.

Cover design by Alan Greco Design.
Cover illustration by Lenny Long. Copyright ©1996.

Library of Congress Cataloging-in-Publication Data

Sophomores : tales of reality, conflict, and the road by tenth grade writers / edited by Christine Lord.
      p.   cm. -- (The American teen writer series)
      Summary: A collection of short stories on various topics, all written by American teenage writers in the tenth grade.
      ISBN 1-886427-10-0
      1. Short stories, American.   2. Youths' writings, American.
[1. Short stories. 2. Youths' writings.]   I. Lord, Christine.
II. Series.
PZ5.S698   1997
[Fic]--dc20   96-25028
                                                                  CIP
                                                                  AC

99 98 97 96   6 5 4 3 2 1

Sophomores

TALES OF REALITY, CONFLICT, AND THE ROAD
BY TENTH GRADE WRITERS

Edited by
Christine Lord

The American Teen Writer Series
Editor: R. James Stahl

Merlyn's Pen, Inc.
East Greenwich, Rhode Island

Acknowledgments

Jo-Ann Langseth, copy editor, is gratefully acknowledged for her significant work in preparing these manuscripts for original publication in *Merlyn's Pen: The National Magazines of Student Writing*.

The American Teen Writer Series

Young adult literature. What does it mean to you?

Classic titles like *Lord of the Flies* or *Of Mice and Men*—books written by adults, for adult readers, that also are studied extensively in high schools?

Books written for teenagers by adult writers admired by teens—like Gary Paulsen, Norma Klein, Paul Zindel?

Shelves and shelves of popular paperbacks about perfect, untroubled, blemish-free kids?

Titles like *I Was a Teenage Vampire*? *Lunch Hour of the Living Dead*?

The term "young adult literature" is used to describe a range of exciting literature, but it has never accounted for the stories, poetry, and nonfiction actually written by young adults. African American literature is written by African Americans. Native American stories are penned by Native Americans. The Women's Literature aisle is stocked with books by women. Where are the young adult writers in young adult literature?

Teen authors tell their own stories in *Merlyn's Pen: The National Magazines of Student Writing*. Back in 1985 the magazine began giving young writers a place for their most compelling work. Seeds were planted. Now, the American Teen Writer Series brings us the bountiful, rich fruit of their labors.

Older readers might be tempted to speak of these authors as potential writers, the great talents of tomorrow. We say: Don't. Their talent is alive and present. Their work is here and now.

About the Author Profiles:

The editors of the American Teen Writer Series have decided to reprint the author profiles as they appeared in *Merlyn's Pen* when the authors' works were first published. Our purpose is to reflect the writers' school backgrounds and interests at the time they wrote these stories.

Contents

Cat Burglary 101.

The Great Egg-Heist

by MARK WENHAM

I was about five years old at the time, dashing and suave in a five-year-old sort of way, and on a mission—a serious mission. It wasn't quite an international espionage thriller, but for me, a five-year-old, it was risking everything. I was gambling all my chips, the whole pie. I was walking a very thin line over the infernal pit of ultimate disaster. This, of course, is a flashy way of saying that I was hazarding a good spanking. Or the loss of TV for a week, which is very serious business.

Ever since I can remember, and long before that, my parents and I have gone up to New Hampshire two or three times every year to visit one of my dad's best friends, a huge lug of a big-hearted German named Bobby Emmel. Despite a hulking, imposing appearance, he was actually one of the gentlest, funniest, kindest, and craziest men that I have ever known; we affectionately called him Fritzy. Every November we would go up for a week, and while my dad and Fritzy went deer hunting, Fritzy's wife, Charlotte, and my mom and I would cruise around, outlet-hopping and playing tennis. Outlets were an incredible bore to me, as shopping, at that age, was not a top-priority activity in life. Cartoons and chasing the cat into the attic were more my style. Charlotte, just as kind and gentle as Fritzy, and considerably smaller, could and still can talk wallpaper off walls. But I wouldn't have her any other way than she is.

Fritzy and Char owned this house in Madison, New Hampshire; that's one of my favorite places in the world. Onto the house, which was built in the 1800s, Fritzy had added a new part that included a large kitchen and the greatest living room I'd ever been in. The huge living room had an immense stone fireplace that Fritzy and I spent hours throwing paper airplanes into, which often flustered Charlotte, as we wasted a lot of paper with our imaginary, fireplace-doomed kamikaze jet fighters. The living room had huge windows everywhere that stretched up to a slanted, massive-beamed ceiling, and it had a red- and black-specked shag rug, plants all over the place, a sofa and seats by the fireplace, huge wooden shelves holding ancient *Reader's Digest*s, books about nature, and an enormously enjoyable remote-control TV. The living room was also tastefully decorated with stuffed trophies from Fritzy's many years of hunting: a fox, a raccoon, moose and deer heads, racks of antlers, a forty-five-pound bass, a weasel, an otter, a bear head, and a swordfish mounted on the stone chimney of the fireplace.

Attached to the house was an old barn-garage that

was a feast for a young imagination. It came complete with dark corners; saggy beams and ceiling; piles of dateless crud; light beams slanting through dirt-encrusted windows into the fine, airborne sediment common to such old places; a distinct, musty odor; and warped, slanted floors that creaked just the right way when walked on. Out in the backyard was a small man-made pond that Fritzy put in when he built the new part of the house. Partially surrounded by brooding willow trees and overlooked by the living room, there were about twelve ducks in it that Charlotte raised and which I fed bread to whenever I was there.

But most important, between the pond and the barn-garage and within view of the living room, was the main attraction—that which occupied most of my time when I visited Fritzy's. The thing which I had a special love for among everything at Fritzy and Char's could completely fascinate any little kid. It was the chicken coop. Yes, the chicken coop. Two rooms connected by a door, easily large enough to walk around in, it had nest boxes all along the walls in one room and three roosts and the feed bin in the other. A tall fence with two doors stretched around one side of the coop to form a rectangular little yard. The doors were mostly open during the day so that the chickens could wander around the backyard and under a good part of the barn, which was on stilts in the back. Naturally, being a kid and small enough, I often wandered around under the barn with them.

I spent a lot of time in that cobweb-covered coop, collecting eggs, getting chicken poop on my shoes, overfeeding the chickens, and just generally bumming around with them. I was the cat's meow when I was with those Rhode Island Reds. I really can't explain my attachment to them. Let it suffice to say that chickens and I were simply destined to be together. And this is where my mission comes into the plot.

I wanted chickens of my own, and I was clueless as to how to go about getting them. They didn't sell live chickens at the supermarket, and planting a dead one from my mother's refrigerator wouldn't make a live one grow. (I determined this from scientific experimentation in my backyard.) I had talked to my dad and he gently told me no, we couldn't get any chickens. Well, the desire to have chickens was burning in me, and I knew with a fateful certainty that I was going to have to do something devious and underhanded to fulfill my wishes. So, one day, late in the afternoon, I was hanging loose with the chickens in the coop, pondering my predicament, when the proverbial bulb went off in my head and a daring scheme hatched. It involved the hijacking of a few eggs.

Setting the plan in motion, I stepped casually outside of the coop to check the backyard and the surrounding area, whistling innocently and looking mellow. On a mission such as this, impeccable composure is a must. And caution often means the difference between life and death. No one was in sight.

I reentered the coop and glanced right and then left through calmly slitted eyes. I was the epitome of a cool cat in motion. I strolled over to the nest boxes, still whistling. Nodding coolly like James Bond would to three or four chickens, I glanced at what was in the nest boxes. A total of four eggs. The tension started to build, soon to become pure, blistering suspense. Something creaked behind me and I whirled, ready either to eliminate the intruder or to look as if nothing were going on. Luckily, it was only a chicken that had jumped into this room from the other one. Being a self-proclaimed master of all that pertains to martial arts, I was a veritable five-year-old death wish to anyone who might have accidentally stumbled onto my operation. Just to be sure that I was still safe, I checked the yard again. Safety is utmost in this business, up there with caution.

Again, I strolled nonchalantly back to the egg boxes. Most five-year-olds, not possessing the finesse that I did, would have simply walked, or stumbled, but I strolled. I briefly flirted with the notion that the chickens in the coop were potentially dangerous witnesses to my crime, but I dismissed this. Chickens can't talk or write or speak in sign language, so there would not be any problem. Besides, twelve mysteriously dead chickens was not the way to eliminate possible suspicion. Anyhow, I paused in front of the boxes, listened, and then quickly slipped all four eggs into the front of my shirt. Stage One completed. The next step was to get the eggs into the house and upstairs, without being noticed, to the room that I always stayed in. No mean task, mind you.

You see, my plan was simply to "borrow" some eggs and hatch them, so that I could have chicks which would, in fact, grow into chickens. Despite the simplicity of the plan, the magnitude of the danger involved in the execution was astounding. Of course, the plan ultimately entailed my parents realizing that I was raising chickens; but, like any good agent, I decided to face that hazard when I came to it. In this business, the immediate danger demands all the attention and concentration one can manage. I sneaked into the barn, bent over trying to protect the eggs in my shirt front, but looking, as always, cool and casual. I found a small paper bag and carefully put the eggs into it. Having no other choice, I planned to carry the bag in full view, which meant that I would have to divert everyone's attention somehow as I slipped upstairs. Being a glutton for thrills and excitement, I decided to completely wing it on the diversion action.

Suddenly, the door connecting the house and the barn opened. Like a hair-trigger pin, I dove behind a pile of crud to conceal myself, landing with the bag held in the air so that the eggs wouldn't crack.

Accidentally, I knocked a toolbox off a workbench and it fell to the floor, spilling tools with a great clatter. Overall, the move wasn't as quiet as I would have liked, but otherwise it was well-executed. I waited silently. Beads of perspiration formed on my forehead. I heard the person empty some trash into a trash can. Ten seconds went by. Twelve. Fifteen. Then I heard the door close. I sighed, waited a moment, took a deep breath, and proceeded into the house. This is where the blistering suspense kicks in.

I walked calmly into the kitchen where my mom and Charlotte were cooking something. My nose immediately detected it to be food, of the soup persuasion. Before they could inquire about the paper bag, I thought fast, pointed at the stove, and said with much alarm in my voice, "The pot's boiling over!" They bought it and looked, and I bolted for the stairs, silently congratulating myself on an immense, powerful diversionary tactic. The most dangerous part of the mission was over. As I passed the bathroom at the top of the stairs, it occurred to me that the bathroom was an ideal place to hang out while the incident downstairs involving the pot and apparent lie concerning it blew over and was forgotten. Plus, I could use what the bathroom had to offer.

Ten minutes and one very thorough egg inspection later, I was ready to terminate the mission. All that remained was putting the eggs inside two socks and wrapping them in several layers of paper towels. Knowing that the eggs needed heat, I judged the socks and paper towels sufficiently warm to hatch them. I left the package in the bottom of my suitcase to incubate in peace and, fully confident that I would soon have my chicks, proudly praised myself on a seamless, immaculately pulled-off mission. It had been risky, but it was worth it.

Nevertheless, when I went back to my room an hour later to see if the eggs had hatched yet, I received an incredibly shocking blow to my senses. What I pulled out of the socks were not eggs or chicks, but four red peppers. Something had gone horribly wrong! My mission, so jubilantly successful only an hour before, had somehow drastically twisted and backfired. All the danger, all the risk involved, and my precious eggs, soon to be chicks, had turned into red peppers. If they had changed into solid chocolate Easter bunnies, or something in that vein, it might have been different. But red peppers?! Thus, I became the unhappy victim of a new biological learning experience, and for many years afterward I lived under the delusion that eggs turn into red peppers when wrapped in two socks and several layers of paper towels.

Later that evening, I slouched downstairs to the living room and sat in the seat that my dad normally occupied. I looked mournfully out the huge windows at the precious chicken coop. It wasn't until years later that the view from this seat dawned on me.

I thought about organizing another mission but decided against it, because there was some secret to hatching eggs that I wasn't privy to. So I made it my next mission to discover this secret and bust it wide open. And when I did . . .

In any case, I quietly gave the peppers to Charlotte, cleverly saying that I had picked them off the willow tree near the chicken coop. I watched her put them in the refrigerator next to some other peppers that looked suspiciously similar. Then I became deeply absorbed in the boldness and complexity of life, the cruelty of it, that it should so maliciously throw a demonic twist of fate into the face of such an innocent, upstanding five-year-old, of all the vulnerable people. I was so absorbed that I didn't notice the mock seriousness with which everyone at dinner talked about the egg count being down. Nor did I notice the entertained, not quite restrained smirks plastered all over everyone's face, especially when they looked at me, listlessly picking at my food. I didn't suspect a thing. But then, agents are people, too. We're not perfect—close, though, very close.

ABOUT THE AUTHOR

Mark Wenham is from Connecticut and attends Tabor Academy, in Marion, Massachusetts. Besides writing and literature, his interests include hockey, skiing, and movies.

People point at him and say, "There's
the son of our lunatic king."

Curse of the Sea Lord

by TRICIA OWENS

S ay one word, Prince Cathmor thought angrily, *and
I'll feed you your tongue.* He glared at the guard
expectantly, almost hopefully, but the guard said
nothing. Yet even as the prince passed by, he sensed a
silent defiance in the guard's rigid stance. The gray-
green eyes that stared from within the visored helmet
appeared to burn with accusation. And the man's hands,
curled firmly about his spear, seemed to quiver, as if
wanting to point suddenly at Cathmor and cry, *There
he is! The son of our lunatic king. See how he glares
with that wild light in his eyes? There's a bit of his father's madness in him already!*

"Fools!" The young prince scowled. They were all
traitors, he decided, as he strode up the hill to the
cliffs. When he became king, things would be different. No more whispering servants and glaring soldiers
when he came to power!

He topped the rise with an eager jump and was

21

buffeted by the chill breath of the sea roaring its greetings to him. The fresh wind blew his clothes tight against his body, and the tangy taste of salt fell upon his lips. Screaming gulls circled overhead while, down below, sleek-bodied seals glistened on the rocks. Cathmor grinned hugely. He loved the sea. For a while he could almost forget the troubles he had left at the castle. Almost. He could sense his father's soldiers, camped several yards away, watching him with wary eyes.

Resisting the urge to berate them, he traversed the path that wound down the cliffside to the beach. The sand beneath his bare feet was warm, and the incessant roaring of the waves sought to soothe him. Still feeling hotheaded, he strode out to the water, determined to walk off the black mood that threatened to overcome him.

His temper had steadily worsened these days. He told himself it was the strain of war. In truth, though, Cathmor himself would have no great role in the anticipated war. At the first sign of trouble he would be spirited to a safehold. No, he wasn't worried about the war. His problems stemmed from another source: his father. If only the king knew how much trouble he caused for his son by acting the way he did! The king's maniacal obsession with the boat he was building—and during a time of imminent war!—made it clear why he was thought to be mad. Certainly no normal king would—

Cathmor stumbled and almost fell as his feet tangled with the body of a man lying half in and half out of the water. Gaping in astonishment, the prince bent over and turned the man onto his back. As he did so, he let out a small cry of disgust. The man's pale blue skin was slimy and covered with thin scales that came off on Cathmor's hands. Further scrutiny of the body showed that the man/thing had large eye sockets, wide nostrils, and a thin webbing of skin between fingers and toes. Cathmor tried to suppress a shudder. This thing on the ground was a Sea Child.

Cathmor had been raised on the terrifying tales of the Sea Children—how they'd steal babies from the coastal towns and drown the unfortunate fishermen who accidentally caught Sea Children in their nets. These strange denizens of the deep were said to be ungodly creatures that took pleasure in tormenting the humans they captured. Looking down on the Sea Child at his feet, Cathmor was filled with mixed emotions of fear and hatred.

For once, though, fear overrode the anger in the young prince. He took a slow step backward, then another, and was about to turn and run when a scaled hand grabbed his ankle with a sickening slap.

The Sea Child's black eyes were enormously round, seeming to bore into Cathmor's soul. "Please . . . help me!"

Cathmor shrieked and tried to jerk his ankle free. Wounded though the creature might be, its grip was unbreakable.

Panicking, Cathmor dragged them both out of the water toward land. He kicked frantically, hoping the stinging sand would force the Sea Child to let go. The steel fingers around his ankle remained firm, but the creature began making retching sounds and thrashed where it lay, its alien face distorted even more.

The realization that the Sea Child was choking filled Cathmor with triumph. He bent eagerly and threw great handfuls of sand over the creature's face, reveling in the sounds he heard. He shoveled more and more sand until, at last, the Sea Child's hand fell slack and its body no longer twitched.

The prince stepped back, elated; then the full impact of what he'd just done turned him cold with disbelief. He nudged the Sea Child with his toe, praying the creature would sit up, unharmed, and return to the sea. But the body didn't move. It was dead. He'd killed it.

"Nooo!" Cathmor's scream tore from his throat and was joined by the wail of the sea. The prince collapsed on the sand and lay there, eyes wide to the sky.

What seemed hours later, Cathmor stood up and calmly dragged the Sea Child back into the water. The prince felt strangely distant, as if he were watching himself hide the body and was not actually doing it. From this strange view, he saw himself run blindly from the beach toward the castle, while behind him the sea became turbulent and its waves tore at the cliffs. He saw how his face was contorted with madness, how the people he passed drew back in fear. He was out of control, running from the invisible terror that lapped at his heels . . .

The prince looked around himself in a daze. With a shock, he realized that he was back in his chambers at the castle. Vaguely, as if from a dream, he remembered only fragments of his nightmare flight. Yet the pieces were enough to remind Cathmor of all that had taken place earlier. He moved to the window and looked out to sea.

The water was wild. Its once-glassy surface was now broken by rearing whitecaps that whipped across the water with horrendous speed. The waves were as high as the base of the cliffs, tearing at their sides like some carnivorous beast, ripping the flesh away. Above the churning waters the darkening sky was thick with gray clouds. Fog crept in like slow fingers to create an eerie, distorted seascape. Gusting winds carried the sea spray up to the castle windows with the force of rain, and throughout the cold-stoned fortress the wind wailed a lament for the lost Sea Child.

Cathmor jerked away from the window and turned his back on the stormy scene. Fear and desperation gripped his heart like a fist. It was all his fault! He'd brought the wrath of the sea upon his father's kingdom, and soon they would all be paying for it.

The prince's eyes darted to the door as the handle rattled. He was hoping he'd remembered to lock it, when the latch clicked and the door swung open to reveal his father, the king, standing in the doorway.

As always when he saw his father, Cathmor felt torn by resentment and pity. This spindly old man with his stooping shoulders and weathered face was the very reason why Cathmor's life was miserable. Though the king's sharply etched features gave him an alert appearance, his unfocused gray eyes betrayed his madness.

Cathmor was sorry to see him.

"One of the servants said you were ill," the king began hesitantly. His gnarled fingers twisted in agitation. "Would you like me to get you something?"

Cathmor's forced smile turned into a grimace. "No. I just need to rest."

The older man nodded and looked around the sparsely decorated room as if searching for something to talk about to fill the awkward silence. Cathmor saw him notice the spray-splattered window and move to it, looking out.

"The sea is angry today," he murmured in a quiet voice. "Someone has wronged it."

Cathmor held his breath, wondering if the king knew about the Sea Child. "It's just storm-struck," he suggested. He feigned nonchalance. "It will die down, I'm certain."

The king turned from the window and shook his head at his son. "No, something is wrong. I have done something to make the sea angry with me. Even now the waves have reached the cliff tops; three soldiers have been washed into the depths."

"What?!" Cathmor stared hard at his father and realized the revelation wasn't a product of his madness. *The sea is punishing us,* the prince thought. *What will stop it from carrying away the castle as well?*

His fists clenched. "Father, you have to do something. Have the soldiers build a barrier to keep the waves back. We have to protect ourselves!"

For the briefest of moments, comprehension flickered in the old man's eyes. In that brief instant the king was young again, displaying the raven-dark hair and handsome, brooding face that could have made him Cathmor's twin. Cathmor glimpsed the man his father should be and perhaps once was: strong, wise, kingly. Here was the king Cathmor would have grown to respect. But the moment was painfully brief. The hazy veil pulled back across his eyes, and he was once again the incompetent king Cathmor despised. The man who stood before Cathmor was a madman. A stranger.

"I . . . I must work on my boat," the old king stammered, shuffling to the door. "Work needs to be done."

"Work does need to be done, but you're not doing it. Forget your idiotic boat and be king for once!"

A shake of the head. "I . . . work on the boat. Need to smooth the sides . . ."

Cathmor seized his father's arm. "Listen, old man—" he began. Then his eyes drifted to the king's robe. The rich fur was dusted with wood shavings and dirt, looking as though he'd worn it all day in his workshop. For some reason the sight of his father's disheveled robe made Cathmor laugh—a little too loudly. "It's no use." He pushed the king out the door. "Tell the true king that his son is waiting to meet him. I'm tired of talking to impostors."

The king paused and looked back, his crown tarnished and hanging awkwardly over his bony brow. He looked a thousand years old. "I'm not mad, my son," he whispered.

Cathmor opened his mouth to say something apologetic, then bit his lip and slammed the door in his father's face.

"I hate him! I hate him! I . . . hate *me*!" Cathmor released his grip on his hair and hugged himself, frightened of what he was becoming. *The madness is truly in me*, he despaired. *I have mercilessly killed a wounded creature and tried to pretend it never happened. Now I am trying to seize the crown from my father's head. It doesn't matter that he's mad, he's still the king. My king.* "I am lost," he whispered aloud.

Boom! Cathmor staggered as the floor beneath him shuddered. He could see through the window that the waves had completely washed over the cliffs and were pounding against the castle walls. There was no sign of the soldiers who had previously camped there. Probably scattered across the sea, the prince realized. He deserved to join them . . .

Sudden daring surged through his body, and before he could change his mind, he dashed from the room. His race through the castle was more controlled this time but no less urgent. Time was running out. A thin coat of water had already seeped across the lower floor by the time Cathmor reached the front doors and heaved them open.

Stinging spray and winds struck his body, tearing his breath away and whipping his cape behind him like a wild bird. He shielded his eyes with one hand and slipped and slithered his way through the drenched fields.

By the time he neared what was left of the cliffs, he was bruised and soaked. He paused to look at the maelstrom around him, at the dim outline of the castle in which he had been born, and he allowed a sad smile to cross his dripping face. Shivering, muddied, the wind painful in his ears, Cathmor took a deep breath and announced himself to the raging sea.

"I'm the one you want!" he screamed, the wind shoving his words back down his throat. "I killed your Sea Child. I'm here to pay the price."

A tremendous wave crashed against the rocks a few feet in front of him. Amidst the spray of water that pelted him, Cathmor heard: "Conceited fool! Your offer is not enough!"

The prince stared out at the dark sea, searching for the owner of that intimidating voice. "I am a royal prince," he retorted, feeling absurdly humiliated. "What could be worth more than I?"

"A king."

Cathmor spun, knowing at once whom this voice belonged to. His father stood behind him, swaying in the wind, his fine fur robe now wet and stringy. His knee-high boots were coated with mud, and his knotted hands were cut and bleeding from stumbling against the rocks. The king looked brittle and weak, and yet, Cathmor was astonished to see, he looked saner than he ever had before.

"What are you doing here?" Cathmor demanded. "Go back to the castle. This has nothing to do with you."

Ignoring him, the king turned and bowed slightly to the sea. "Greetings, Sea Lord. I am early but I am prepared to go."

"What is happening?" Cathmor screamed in frustration.

In answer, the king pointed to the sea. Rising from the waves like a newborn emerging from its mother burst the gigantic figure of a man. It drew itself up to tower over father and son like some unreal statue. Cathmor stepped back a pace, awed by this terrible, beautiful creature. Its glistening scaled skin was blue, and its large black eyes and lipless mouth made its face strange and exotic. The creature was powerfully built with arms like tree trunks and a chest and stomach that rippled with muscles. With its fingers the Sea Lord could easily snap a man in twain.

But what caught Cathmor's attention more than the Sea Lord's physical appearance was what the creature wore. A circlet of rose coral rested across the Sea Lord's brow, and around its thickly muscled shoulders lay a dripping robe of woven seaweed. It was this robe that Cathmor's eyes were drawn to, for draped across the robe's front, like a string of decorative jewels, were the shriveled heads of Cathmor's ancestors. Generations of kings who had died at sea now bobbed like parasites on the Sea Lord's robe. The young prince felt his insides recoil as he stared at the severed heads.

"Greetings, King of Rheysdan," the Sea Lord bellowed. Its voice was deep and resonant, as if echoing from within a giant conch shell. "I accept your offer." It swung a hand across the surface of the water and immediately a wave rose, riding in the direction of the docks. "Your boat will be here shortly."

"What offer? What are you talking about?" Cathmor stomped his foot. "I demand to know!"

A thin, cold hand settled upon his shoulder, and the warm breath of his father tickled his ear. "We are caught in a curse, Cathmor—you and I and all past and future kings of Rheysdan Isle. We are trapped on this island because the Sea Lord will devastate Rheysdan if we try to leave it."

"But why are we cursed? Why can't we leave?"

Out in the water the Sea Lord growled and slapped its palm down. "You are cursed because you are sons of that treacherous King Menwyn who stole my beloved!"

"It means that we are descendants of King Menwyn, the first ruler of Rheysdan Isle," Cathmor's father explained. "Hundreds of years ago King Menwyn wooed the Sea Lord's lover from her domain. She gave up her sea life to live as Queen of Rheysdan. Because of this, the jealous Sea Lord set a curse upon King Menwyn. The curse stated that, for all eternity, all future kings of Rheysdan must give their lives to the sea. Not only must they sacrifice themselves, but they must do so in the prime of life, when they are the most powerful, when they are loved the most and will therefore be missed the most. It is the price the Sea Lord demands for its lover's infidelity." The hand on Cathmor's shoulder tightened. "You heard me tell the Sea Lord that I am early. This is true. My time to enter the sea would ordinarily have been weeks from now, the day after the war. That is why I spent no time preparing for the battle. I didn't need to. I was destined to win and become the most powerful king in the Five Isles, to be the most beloved. Now," he smiled gently, "I must meet my death as an unloved and unpopular king. But I am not disappointed."

"No!" Cathmor tore from his father's grip and confronted the Sea Lord. "You can't do this!" he declared, his voice sounding weak and insubstantial even to his own ears. "Who do you think we are? We aren't Menwyn. He died hundreds of years ago."

The Sea Lord shook its head, a great spray of salt water splattering the cliffs. "You carry his blood. As long as he lives, even through you, I must punish him."

The prince laughed bitterly. "You're mad. People say that my father and I are crazy, but it's you who has lost your senses. Do you think you can control our lives? Do you think you hold the knife to our lifeline? Well, you don't, do you hear? We can fight you! Can't we, Father? Father?"

But the king was gone. Cathmor spun fearfully and caught sight of the old man already halfway down the cliffside.

"Stop, Father! Don't go!"

The king paused to wave briefly, then continued to

pick his way down. Cathmor cursed and scrambled down the muddy path, racing to catch up with his father.

He was too late. Already the old man was on the beach, running with amazing agility to where a boat was being carried by the waves to the shore. It was his funeral boat. Cathmor halted in disbelief as he stared at the project his father had committed almost a year to building. It was a dull, ugly vessel that rested heavily in the water, unfit for proper travel. Its hull was covered with strange dark plates hammered together like a shell of armor. The overall result was amateur-looking, nothing at all like the fantastic boat Cathmor had envisioned. He watched, stunned, as the gloomy, sailless tomb welcomed his father onto her deck.

"Father!"

The king didn't look back. He moved instead to where a torch burned in its holder by the rails. He took the torch and went below into the heart of the boat for a moment and then emerged without the torch.

"Say farewell to your father, King Cathmor!"

The prince couldn't summon a retort as he watched a wave propel the boat into deeper waters. Through his tear-blurred eyes he could see his father standing at the rails, his white hair flying behind him. He was waiting to die, waiting to breathe the dark, salty waters.

"I'm such a fool," Cathmor sobbed aloud, slumping against the rocks. "I have invited my father's death. He will die as I should, and betrayed by the one who should love him most. Forgive me, Father!"

The Sea Lord smiled at his anguished plea. "Say farewell," it repeated.

It extended a giant blue hand down to the miserable boat. As its fingers curled around the hull and lifted it out of the water, it emitted a triumphant laugh.

"King Menwyn, I have bested you again!"

The Sea Lord's strange face twisted with glee. Suddenly, though, it changed to a look of pain. Cathmor pushed to his feet as the Sea Lord howled in an inhuman voice and stared down incredulously at the small boat in its hand. The strange plates covering the hull had turned a bright red, and the deck, where Cathmor's father crouched, was blackening. The Sea Lord screeched again as its fingers began to smoke and blister, and the air was filled with the stench of burning flesh. With an outraged roar, the mighty Sea Lord flung the burning boat toward shore.

As the boat dashed against the cliffs and fell to the beach, Cathmor cried out. There amid the smoking wreckage, he sighted a white form, streaked with red. Heedless of the string of curses streaming from the Sea Lord, he darted toward the wreckage and kneeled beside the broken body of his father.

"I'm so sorry," the young prince sobbed, cradling his father's head in his lap. "If only I'd known about the curse earlier. I—"

His father raised a shaking finger and laid it across his son's lips. "Think no more of what could have been," he whispered. "We are together now as we should be. We are father and son at last. The time before this is forgotten."

Cathmor nodded, tears slipping from his eyes. "We are together." He glanced around him at the smoking coals in the sand. "What did you do?" he asked.

He was rewarded with a weak, bloodstained smile. "I outsmarted the Sea Lord. It never expected a boat plated with metal and heated from the inside with burning coals." The king coughed and his fingers clutched tightly to his crushed chest. "I had hoped the results would be different. I had hoped we could break this curse and escape together. Now you alone must do it."

"I will, Father. I promise." Cathmor dashed the tears from his eyes and bent to kiss his father on one hollowed cheek. "I love you."

The old king smiled and for a moment his face was free of pain. Then his breath whistled between his teeth in a satisfied sigh . . . he was gone. A smile was on the young prince's face as he placed the old man's arms across his chest and stood up.

"They all die one way or another," taunted the Sea Lord.

Cathmor pivoted on his heel and walked with determined steps to the water line. He threw his head back confidently, and the king-light was in his eyes when he stared up at the Sea Lord.

"I can beat you," he declared. "My father beat you and I'll do the same. Only this time you will be the one who dies."

The Sea Lord laughed, but without mirth. "Pitiful mortal! I will take particular delight in your death. You owe me two lives—your own and that of my Sea Child. I will not forget that." Carelessly, the sea creature reached up and plucked one of the heads from its robe. "This is Menwyn," the creature explained. "I will replace his rotted head with your fresh one."

Cathmor ignored the head as it was flicked past him onto the sand. "Hear this: I will escape this island, but you won't be alive to wish me farewell."

"Ho! Is that a challenge I hear?"

Cathmor nodded, and a determined grin spread across his face. "It is a challenge. And keep this in mind, mighty Lord of the Sea: I am a madman. And madmen don't fight fair."

ABOUT THE AUTHOR

Tricia Owens lives in Bakersfield, California, where she attends North High School. Her interests include volleyball, tennis, the violin, and writing. "I love delivering the speeches I've written, not to mention testing out my poetry on any sympathetic ear I can find."

Why couldn't she have a normal life?
Why was *she* responsible for her brother?

My Brother, My Heart

by NANCY O'NEALE

I sang along with the choir as they led the church into the hymn. I so much wanted to be a choir member, to be in the bliss unison, but I believed I never would. My brother, my best friend, stuttered, and I could never be so cruel as to leave him and sit with the people in the loft. It was a mistake for me to even be singing. This was Riley's most nervous time in the church service. To block out the noise of the choir, I examined the celestial building and all the people in it. It had five, six—no, seven stained-glass windows. The light shone through the apse in the summer. The benches were of hard maple wood. My brother and I were sitting between my grandmother and mother. The people in the loft were now in their seats. The preacher took his stand behind the sturdy pulpit.

"Time to go to sleep," I whispered to my brother.

"Ree-Ree, hush your mouth!" hissed my stone-faced mother.

The pastor had started his sermon. "God is no respecter of persons." I thought he preached this same sermon last week. It seemed like he preached the same sermon every week. Either that or the whole Bible blended in together. As soon as we left the wooden edifice, I knew my mother would not forget my misbehavior of speaking in church.

"For your disobedience both of you will walk home."

Even Mama must have perceived that this was more of a blessing than a punishment. Riley and I enjoyed taking long walks. Our distances were challenging, and we always tried to discover new territory. My brother and I held hands as we started the mile-long journey, which was about the same as the distance to school. We stepped over plenty of rocks, *crush, stomp, crush, stomp,* on the dirt road and hardly spoke. When we reached home, my stockings were a bit discolored, but my brother remained spotless. We sat down on the worn-out porch, licking cherry-lemonade Popsicles and watching my grandmother sway in her rocking chair while sipping her tart-tasting lemonade.

The next morning, like all mornings, Greenville woke up to a chilling dew-mist instead of sun. The coldness of the bitter dawn was hard to suffer for my brother and me as we walked the mile to school. We didn't hold hands. He said that only Sunday should be reserved for showing affection. I worried that it might make me look less than my seventeen years to be walking with a little kid and holding his hand, but I never told him this.

Even though I was an honor student, beyond boredom, I felt resentment during classes. If God is no respecter of persons, then why did the Negro schools have secondhand books and the white kids receive new books with fresh covers and uncut pages?

Why were some sick and some well? Why were few rich and most poor? That's what we were, dirt poor. Although my mother often camouflaged it, the fact of our indigence still remained. My crisp-ironed, home-made dresses and my brother's clean striped suit did not make up for the frequent greens and cornbread dinners. If God is no respecter of persons, then how come my brother stuttered and I spoke clearly? Before my thoughts were finished, we had arrived at school.

After school it was time to walk over the tarred concrete and behind the fence to the elementary section where I picked up Riley. My brother dashed out of his seat to hug me.

"Why are you so excited, Riley?"

"I saw s-snow!"

What?! He saw snow. One thing I knew is that it never snowed in Greenville, or if it had, it hadn't snowed today. The dawns were bitter cold, but the vermilion dirt in the afternoon was enough to make the soles of your shoes melt.

"It doesn't snow in Greenville, Riley," I retorted.

"I uh-know that," he said matter-of-factly. "We-we saw a m-m-movie in c-c-class on-on-on nature!" He stopped to take a breath. "It's the most bu-bu-bu-beautiful stuff I've ever s-s-s-seen!"

I doubted that he'd ever see snow unless a storm came to Greenville. My grandmother and mother were born here and they never left. They'd been to Savannah a couple of times to pick peaches to make peach nectar and peach jam. I wondered if Riley would ever leave Greenville. I hoped to receive a scholarship from some small black college. My father lived in Chicago. He would never allow Riley to visit. He didn't want any handicapped children; he considered Riley's stuttering a handicap. I'd seen snow a couple of times.

"I wa-wa-wanna s-s-see some snow!"

Now he was whining. He hadn't whined since he was a baby and I couldn't stand it then. Riley was not my full responsibility. Momma would have to take care of this.

"We'll talk to Momma when we get home," I said in a restrained voice.

We took the path home that we had recently discovered. Riley babbled as well as he could about the snow. I kept saying that we would discuss it with Mother. The silence of the bronze earth was much as it was on Sunday afternoon. The heat only changed with the seasons, except for an occasional rainfall.

A car slowing alongside us soon broke the silence. They had their convertible top down. Riley was on the outside of me and they might try to spit on him. I pulled him over and we switched sides. *Crunch, stomp, crunch, stomp,* our pace increased. They continued to follow with snickers and chuckles among them. One white leaned out of a car door.

"N-N-N-Nigger!"

The word rang in my mind. I reached into the bronze earth and picked up what lay there. I threw it with all my strength. The car was a little way in front of us, and I hit that white boy in the back of his blond head. The rock had been my friend. The tawny dust had been a companion.

"You-you-you-you h-h-hit him, R-Ree! You hit him!"

The snickers turned into shock as they sped away.

Curiosity had risen in me: How did that white boy know my brother stuttered? I knew the remark was targeted more to my brother than me. We couldn't tell Momma about this.

"We're going to find a different route to school," was all I said. My brother was still rejoicing when suddenly he ceased.

"Why did they c-c-c-call me a n-n-n-nigger?" Incredulous concern mixed with the cracked impairment that would never heal. "I-I c-can't help it if I-I-I'm a nigger!"

"Oh, Riley, you're not a nigger. You are not a nigger . . ."

I held my brother tight. I had to keep myself strong so that he wouldn't fall apart. I walked the rest of the way home asking myself how to explain racism and bigotry to a seven-year-old, knowing we'd be embraced by it for the rest of our lives.

Later that night Riley came into my room while I was sleeping. He had a temper tantrum.

"I wa-wanna see some s-s-snow! I wa-wa-wanna see some s-s-snow! . . ." At his every demand he made a crescendo of uproar.

I thought about slapping him into silence, but I knew I could never hit my brother. I'd promised Riley he'd discuss the snow this evening with his momma. Where was his mother, anyway? Always working, always working. Couldn't she take time to raise her children? Why couldn't he leave me alone!

"Riley, be quiet before you wake Grandmother! I told you it doesn't snow in Greenville."

"I can go ta Chi-Chi-Chi-cago! You went ta Chi-Chi-Chi-cago! I can h-h-h-hitchhike," he grimaced. "I know my d-d-daddy loves me jus-just as much as he loves you!"

I couldn't believe he was comparing me to himself. He didn't understand that Dad was a respecter of persons. I rose out of my bed.

"You hitchhike, boy, and you're going to come back with a rope around your neck hanging on a tree."

"I-I'm gonna pack now, to start my t-trip . . ." He had a rascally grin on his face, as if he had outsmarted me. I caught him by his pajama sleeve and dragged him to the kitchen where his voice echoed. I opened the icebox to let my head cool off and took out the cherry-lemonade Popsicles because I knew they were his favorite. I don't know what I planned to do with the Popsicles. Maybe I was going to succor my brother, as if giving candy to a baby.

Instead, I yanked the toothpicks out of the ice trays, emptying the trays onto our good wooden cutting board. I searched for the potato masher in the silverware drawer and crushed the Popsicles . . . I was going to give him some snow, all right! I scooped it all up and then threw the crushed ice into his face. My grandmother was standing in the kitchen doorway. She picked up her plump "picking" hand and slapped me hard. The right side of my sheepish face throbbed. Numbness, just like my frozen fingers.

"Clean up this mess and go to bed!" she bellowed.

"Yes, ma'am," I whispered.

Why was I the one to be slapped? Why did I have to suffer the consequences when my brother was the one who was so stubborn and annoying? I heard water running in the bathroom, and I knew Riley was washing his face for the second time tonight. I felt a bitter hatred for my brother, for that white boy, for everyone.

This just wasn't fair. I was seventeen and had never even been to the movies. I wanted to be in the church choir. I wanted friends to go to the ice cream parlor with. I wanted a normal life, and I didn't want a brother who stuttered. The word "stutter" made me shiver.

The air in the kitchen became too thin. I took off my nightgown, put on a crisp-ironed white dress, and went through the back door to the side of the house. I started to shake and shiver without a sound from my mouth. Stuffy tears came out into the darkness, striking the tawny dust and coloring it vermilion. I wanted to reshape my life in this clay. I rolled around in the yellow-red substance until my dress was fully dirty. I chased all the virtue out of me, and now I was satisfied. Once back in my shelter, my bedroom, I took off my moist, wrinkled dress and climbed into bed. I didn't even wash my face.

About the Author

Nancy O'Neale lives in Atlanta, Georgia, and attends Wayland Academy in Beaver Dam, Wisconsin. She reports that basketball, writing, and lecturing about black history to fellow students occupy much of her time. She wrote and submitted this story while at Hebron Academy in Hebron, Maine.

Was it too late to take back his wish?

Harry's Hurried Childhood

by ALAN MCCABE

I'm real depressed, Doc," Harry Quickman told his psychiatrist. He seemed nervous and on edge, frequently running his sweaty hands through his hair.

"Let us talk then," replied the psychiatrist, a soft-spoken, calm man who wore a brown suit. The two men sat face to face, the doctor behind a neat and orderly desk, the patient on a cushioned seat. This setup would often become uncomfortable for Harry during the sessions. When those droopy, brown eyes of the psychiatrist began staring into his own, they seemed to be probing his innermost thoughts, boring into his mind and catching everything that was not said. At these times, Harry had to get up and pace about the small, windowless room.

"I'm depressed because I didn't have a childhood," said Harry.

"You told me that before," said the psychiatrist, "but you've never told me exactly what you mean by it." The eyes probed deeper. "You never had a pet, perhaps? You never had any true friends? Your parents were cruel?"

The eyes probed deeper still with each question. Harry stood up and walked back and forth.

"No, Doc, I never had a childhood! Oh, how do I tell you? I've never explained it to you before because I knew you'd think I was crazy. But I gotta tell somebody. Sit back in that chair, Doc; it's a long and bizarre story . . .

"As a kid, I loved Christmas—I absolutely loved it! But for all the childish and selfish reasons: receiving toys and candy, stuffing myself at Christmas Eve dinner, going out to play in the snow, being the center of attention when all the relatives visited. I would look forward to Christmas all year, always wanting everything else to be over and done with so Christmas would come again. My Christmas list was always written by June. As the months went on, I would make so many revisions and additions that by December it would be at least twenty pages long. Every year it was the same. In January I wished there were some way to speed up the year, just so it would be December 25 again.

"One of my favorite Christmas treats was the annual visit from Uncle Titus. He was a peculiar fellow. He traveled extensively and always came back with odd souvenirs from his voyages abroad. Well, on the Christmas which found me at the age of six, Christmas 1949, Uncle Titus presented to me a souvenir which was perhaps the most magnificent of any he'd ever given me. However, because of my selfish eagerness, it turned out to be the most horrible, for it caused me to be deprived of my childhood.

"I remember it all very vividly. I guess that's because it's just about the only childhood memory I can claim. We were all sitting around the tree, the whole family; wrapping paper was strewn about the floor. All my new toys were around me like a mighty fortress. Only a handful of unopened presents remained under the tree.

" 'Where's my present from you, Uncle Titus?' I asked eagerly.

"He took a small wrapped package out of the breast pocket of his plaid pajamas and handed it to me.

" 'It's so little!' I said.

" 'Big things come in small packages,' my infinitely wise uncle remarked.

"I ripped the brown paper wrapping from the parcel; I then had in my hand a small wooden box painted with bright swirling colors—the spiraling design seemed to be turning round and round before my very eyes. A small metal clasp kept the box shut. I unhooked it and looked in the box. I saw nothing.

" 'Uncle Titus, it's empty!' I whined.

" 'Look again, m'boy!'

"I did. And again, I saw nothing. By this I mean absolutely nothing! It was completely black inside that tiny colorful box; looking into it was like looking through a window to outer space. I was about to thrust my whole hand into that box to see if I could pull anything out, but my uncle grabbed my arm, saying, 'No! No! You must let it come to you, Harry!' So I waited quite a while, growing more doubtful by the minute. My mom and dad came to my side. They became as mesmerized as I was by the black void within the box. After many minutes, something began to happen. I could hear a faint whisper, or a hiss—it seemed to be saying something, but quietly and in a foreign language. It grew steadily louder. I then saw a small speck of blue. It was far away in this blackness I was looking into, but it was steadily approaching. Closer and closer this cloud of blue came, getting bigger and bigger. 'Oh my God,' I heard my father, still by my side, whisper.

"Now the blue cloud was at the very edge of the black void, and it swirled around in circles, just like the design on the box. Round and round it went until it began to rise slowly out of the box, heading right for my face! It became thin and bore a resemblance to a fine blue thread. Suddenly, the string of blue smoke darted toward me. I felt a sudden pang of terror as that blue smoke, now more like blue lightning, shot at my face. I opened my mouth to scream—and into my open mouth went the smoke! I felt it go down my throat.

"Trembling, I looked up at Uncle Titus. I could say nothing. Mom and Dad could not speak either. Their faces showed the same fear I felt. Dad finally found his voice and said to his brother (not at all in a voice of approval, either), 'You've really outdone yourself this time, Titus.'

"Uncle Titus patted my head and laughed and said, 'What'd ya think o' that, m'boy? Heh, heh! Now listen close. That was the Blue Smoke of Jooba. I picked it up in Egypt. Make a wish, Harry, and it will come true! Plus (and this is what makes the Blue Smoke of Jooba the finest of all the wishbringers), the smoke is in you now—it's a part of you! It will always be with you. Anytime you make that same wish, it'll still come true!'

"Every child's fantasy! Make a wish and it will come true! Well, one and only one thought came automatically to my mind about what my one wish would be. In my selfish little head, I came up with a brilliant plan. Looking at my pile of toys, I pictured it twice as high . . . thrice as high . . . towering up to the sky high! No more would I have to wait for Christmas! I would bring Christmas to me!

" 'I wish it were Christmas 1950!' I said. Everything became pitch-black around me, and I felt like I was floating through some kind of thick ooze. I heard the voices of my parents, my friends, even myself—but I could see nothing. I then had the sensation of falling, and I landed lightly on our living room floor. The next thing I knew, there was a whole mess of unopened Christmas presents around me. I quickly got down to business! My greedy little fingers dove into the shiny red wrappings, unraveled the rosy ribbons, bit and tore into the papered parcels, making the sounds I looked forward to all year round: *Ssshhhhk! Ffffft! Rrrrrip!* Soon there was a pile of paper on one side of me and a tower of toys on the other . . . Teddy bears and bright-colored bouncy balls! Candy canes and Candyland! Chocolate Santas and Chinese checkers! Two toy guns and a talking clock! Everything but a partridge in a pear tree. I was in Christmas heaven!

"My family was there, too, of course; it was just like a normal Christmas at the Quickmans'. After opening my presents, I went outside to play in the snow a bit and showed off in front of my aunts and uncles. When the day was over, I wanted Christmas again. I said, 'I wish it were Christmas 1951!'

"I again made that strange journey through darkness and landed in Christmas 1951. And once again, we repeated all our family Christmas traditions—except the one in which we danced around the tree while Bing Crosby sang 'The Little Drummer Boy' on the scratchy record player and then all joined in our 'family hug.' Mom always insisted we do this before we opened any presents, and it drove me insane with anticipation. As we dipped and twirled beneath the tree, I always became dizzy and could not keep my eyes off the enticing collection of gifts. 'Open me! Open me!' they were calling. But all the other Christmas traditions I had no quarrel with: the roast turkey and gravy and mashed potatoes whose delightful aroma filled the house from noon till midnight . . . Aunt Louella telling one of her stories, which were completely pointless and didn't even have a punch line but were great to listen to just the same. All these things I loved. I truly seemed to think they were the only things I loved. And so I skipped over everything else—over and over again, until Christmas 1959—just to get to these moments. Somehow I just did not realize that similar lovely moments occur throughout life, any time of the year.

"I had a huge pile of toys by now indeed, but I suddenly felt unbelievably tired and sad. I was now sixteen years old, and, in my mind, getting toys and playing in the snow did not mean as much to me. Although all the Quickmans were present at each of the Christmases, I had this feeling of missing my family very much. I felt as if I had lost a lot of time that could have been spent with them. And indeed I had! I yearned, for the first time ever, for all the big and little joys that everyday life brings. So I spent all of Christmas 1959, and every day thereafter, with my family. But I was very confused: my family acted as if I had never been gone—as if I had spent the last ten years with them—but I had no memory of it! To me, those ten years had been spent zipping through time and space—nonexistent to me! I had no memory of those years at all! And yet, I had the knowledge and sense of a normal sixteen-year-old.

"So there you have it, Doc. Through a selfish, childish whim, I expunged an entire decade of my existence, perhaps the ten most influential, enjoyable years of a person's life. And I can't get them back. I want to have—or to have had—a childhood!"

"That's a very interesting story," said the psychiatrist.

"But you don't believe it, and you think I'm a loony-bird," said Harry.

"Well, it seems to me, Harry, that you have two problems here. You are depressed, and you fear that your peers may think you're insane. According to your story, though, one action can solve both problems—wish yourself back to Christmas 1949! The smoke is still with you. You said it granted the same wish every time you wished it. By wishing to return to Christmas 1949, you'd be making basically the same wish as you had so many times before: to go to a different Christmas of your life. Make the wish, Mr. Quickman! Go back to Christmas 1949 and change your original wish . . . Find your childhood."

Harry saw he had nothing to lose. If it worked, he would have his childhood back. If nothing happened, he could laugh and say, "I was only kidding. Had you going there, didn't I?"

He closed his eyes and took a deep breath. "I wish it were Christmas 1949!"

"I'll never forget that Christmas!" proclaimed ancient Uncle Titus at the Quickman dinner table on Christmas Eve. "Christmas 1949! It was nearly forty-five years ago, but I remember it as if it were yesterday. When I gave you that Blue Smoke of Jooba, Harry, I thought for sure you'd wish for something silly like a certain toy you had had on your list but didn't receive. Or maybe a million jillion dollars or something selfish like that. But, no, Harry, m'boy, you got philosophical on us, and I'll never forget it! 'I wish to live every moment of my life to the fullest,' you said, 'by enjoying the love of my family and friends.' Took us all by surprise, ya sure did, m'boy!"

It had taken Harry by surprise when he had said it, too. Even now, almost forty-five years later, he had no idea how a six-year-old boy could possibly have thought up such a wish. However, he would never take that wish back—not for all the toys in the world—because he had lived a full, enjoyable life, a life full of pleasant childhood memories.

ABOUT THE AUTHOR

Alan McCabe lives in West Chester, Pennsylvania, where he attends West Chester East High School. "Writing is my main interest," he reports, but he's also a collector of The Wizard of Oz *memorabilia. He enjoys tennis and writing and performing rock 'n' roll songs.*

Thoughts on a terminal mother . . .

The Airport

by Sanam Roder

E scalators scare me. I heard a story once about a woman who choked when her beads, pearl beads, got stuck in the step. It pulled her closer and closer to the underside of the floor. She died. Wicked and cruel they seem, with teeth that bite you if you miss a step, and a hard rubbery place to rest your hand.

Mom would have flipped if she saw the mess in the airport bathroom. Like a dirty wedding gown, torn to pieces in an awesome fury and thrown about by a bride in underwear and a teary painted face. It's a good thing she doesn't have to see it. She didn't want to come, so she left me alone to wait for that important person.

The airplanes think that they are important, too. They roll around the cement, crossing any lines that seem to have been placed there for a reason. They go real slow, roaring like beasts so as to show off their mighty power. Then they go in circles and make us look at all their sides, their cockpit with a man in a Tupperware hat in the front, and a lot of people, important people, who stick their heads to the windows behind him. The planes always have their behinds uncovered. They flip their tails up and show us everything.

That woman by the Coke machine is weird. She jitters and shakes and even spits. Maybe she's one of those sick people, like Mom says I am. I'm not sick, though. I don't spit. I don't cry, either. I don't like to cry. It makes her mad that I don't cry, even madder than the mailman who won't even walk up to our house. He looked at my mom real funny this morning before I left. He looked at her long and hard and mad. He even looked like he would walk up to her and maybe cuff her like those policemen did last night. He'd have to walk up to our house, though, and I don't think that he's the type to change his ways just because of a crying old woman and her daughter who was leaving for a little while. I'm only going to the airport, I wanted to say, but Mom pushed me into the car before I could yell anything.

These airport hamburgers sure taste bad, and the flight that Mom couldn't remember the number of still hasn't come. I'd rather be eating hamburgers at the neighborhood diner that me and Mom eat at because it has a window that looks straight out onto the runway. The waitress there usually yells at me to hurry up and get out, though. She called me names once and got my mom real mad, so mad that she got out of her seat and punched the woman straight in the nose, real close to the eyes. Blood squirted out and made her look like a candy cane, the kind of candy cane with lots of red and uneven swirls. Mom was really mad. She pulled me from behind the table and took me home and made me look like an even bigger candy cane or maybe one of the hamburgers that hadn't been fried yet.

I can always remember numbers like my phone number or the number that lights up at the bank and tells you how much you're going to sweat that day. Mom said that I shouldn't waste a quarter to call her because she knew where I was. But I have to call her because I saw her picture in a newspaper behind a wire screen. I didn't read the words, though, because it said twenty-five cents, and if I was going to use the quarter that Mom gave me, I might as well call her instead. I guess she isn't waiting because she didn't pick up the phone, and the only other person that could have picked it up is Deirdra May, the dog, but she is probably in the basement.

I guess I could read the words now, but I heard once that those newspaper boxes eat quarters, and I never heard anything like that about gumball machines. Gum does get hard, though, if you chew it for a really long time, and that important person hasn't landed yet, so maybe I'll be chewing it a lot. Maybe chewing slowly will help. It's hard to see things straight when my mouth is opening and closing really far and wide, especially in the dark through a window, looking at big cocky airplanes that aren't going anywhere.

ABOUT THE AUTHOR

Sanam Roder lives in Broomall, Pennsylvania, and wrote this story as a student at Marple Newtown Sr. High School in Newtown Square.

She enjoys the challenge of competing in karate tournaments and "beating arrogant guys who laugh when I ask to spar." Sanam is captain of her JV volleyball team and has played lacrosse for many years. She's also into acting and directing, playing the piano, and writing. She reports: "I want to become a doctor and do research on natural medicines to treat people who are dying of things that have simple cures."

The great escape that almost was . . .

Coward

by DRAKE BENNETT

D rake, you're making this difficult. You know you're going to have to come out sometime, so you might as well get it over with." Mom's voice had grown impatient. The hard asphalt scraped against my bare body as I turned on my stomach to face her. My nose, pressed against the parking lot ground, was filled with the dead stench of aging, worn tires, the fumes of burnt gas and dripping oil. I raised my head, hitting it hard on the metal of the muffler above me. A sharp burst of screaming pain shot through my skull. I peered out from under the car at the two sets of feet that imprisoned me. One I recognized immediately: the creased, black leather heels Mom wore to work every day. The white Reebok walking shoes beside them I assumed belonged to the nurse. Mom was wrong. There was no way I was coming out from under that car. It was all that protected me from the pain and terror I had so recently escaped.

The wind picked up, blowing in gusts, skittering freshly fallen leaves across the pavement. A million tiny goose bumps rose all over my body, and I shivered. I was cold.

Cold. The bed in the examining room had been cold. The nurse had come into the room and told me to strip down to my underwear and sit on the bed. The bed had been soft but rubbery, and cold, cold like the blubbery dead flesh of some whale. The paper covering stuck to the backs of my naked thighs, and I rumpled and creased it each time I shifted my weight.

I was only four now, but I could remember coming to Dr. Castor's office twice before, and I knew what to expect. In a few minutes Dr. Castor himself would come in and do all the "checkup" sorts of things: the poking and probing and tapping and weighing and feeling sorts of things. After he finished, he would talk to my mom for a while and then leave. I would wait for a few more minutes.

Then came the part I dreaded, the part that made my checkups with Dr. Castor hellish. The nurse would walk into the room carrying a bottle of alcohol and a cotton swab and a little plastic bag. I would bare my trembling arm, and she would wet the swab with alcohol. Noticing my clammy palms and tensed face, she would ask if I was scared. I would shake my head quickly; she would smile, a wide, well-rehearsed smile.

"This will only hurt for a second."

Then she would clean off a spot on my upper arm, quickly open the plastic bag, take out the syringe, and plunge it in. In a moment it was over, and she was smiling even more broadly and drawing a smiley face on my arm. Yet there was that split second, that tiny eternity when the needle was in my arm and under my skin, in my flesh, when I was seized with an animal panic, a wave of revulsion and pain and confusion.

I sat on the bed rigidly. The room smelled strongly of medical paraphernalia. I could almost taste the sterile, biting odor of chemicals and latex. I caught myself stroking the flesh of my upper arm absent-mindedly and stopped quickly.

In a few minutes, I heard Dr. Castor's voice outside the door.

"Yep. Well, thanks for coming. See you soon."

The door opened and there he was, just as I had remembered from my appointments before. The same tall frame, the same broad shoulders, the same bright blue eyes.

"Hey there, Tiger, how's it going?" He came over and shook my hand. I felt a little better. Not a lot of people took the trouble to shake the hand of a four-year-old.

"Fine." My smile was weak.

Dr. Castor was quick and efficient. Everything he did he did smoothly and casually. He shined lights in my eyes and ears, felt along my skin, pecked at my knees with his little rubber hammer. He kept up a constant stream of questions, about life at preschool, about what movies I had seen and what my favorite foods were. I answered with a "yes" or "no," not really paying attention to what he was asking.

Just as he was finishing, the door opened and Mom came in. She smiled over at me.

"Soja!" Dr. Castor and my mom always found something to chatter about.

"I was just running some errands; you know how

it is." Mom took her coat off and sat down in one of the blue plastic chairs beside the bed.

"Oh, yeah," Dr. Castor responded. His face melted into an exaggerated look of understanding and sympathy. "Well, that's just about it." He put his little hammer back into the pocket of his lab coat and took off his rubber gloves. "Judy will be in in a moment."

The tension and terror that had been building slowly since I walked into the office had grown stifling. The smiling teddy bears and rabbits on the wall leered cruelly at me. The walls themselves seemed to close in. Every sound of a footstep outside the door made me nearly nauseous with anxiety.

Hours passed before she came. It was the same nurse who had shown me to the room and told me to take off my clothes. She was carrying the bottle and the swab and the bag. I began to shake violently.

Suddenly, madly, I decided to run, to get as far away as I could from this office. I would escape. I considered the options: running was the only viable choice. Adrenaline coursed through me like electricity.

The nurse turned to wet the swab. Still between me and the door, she turned and opened her mouth to say something. I burst past her through the half-open door, down the hallway, and out into the lobby. A scream exploded from my lungs, a scream of terror and panic. Faces, confused and frightened, snapped up from their magazines. I looked down and realized that I was still only wearing my briefs and ran faster— I was nearly flying now. I ran through both sets of double glass doors and stopped in the parking lot. I had no place to go.

Hinges squeaked behind me as I turned to see Mom

and the nurse coming through the first set of doors. Mom's Saab was parked just two rows away. I sprinted for it. I tried the doors; they were locked. I ran around to the other side of the car, dove under it, and scurried out of reach, wincing as the pavement bruised my knees and elbows. I was safe.

They were still waiting, and I was getting very cold. I had not come this far to be so easily trapped. Slowly, silently, I inched my way toward the other side of the car. I looked out, making sure the escape route was clear. Quickly, I got to my feet, still crouching on the opposite side from my two pursuers. Just as I was about to make my break, I heard the tap of footsteps behind me. I whirled to find myself face to face with Mom. I turned and ran, but she was on me. Another set of arms grabbed me as the nurse arrived. They dragged me into the office. I didn't struggle; it was useless. The wave of laughter that swept the waiting room as our grim procession passed through stung me, and I burned with embarrassment.

When we got to the waiting room, Mom held me down while the nurse swabbed my arm. She didn't need to. I wasn't going to try to escape again. The nurse gave me the shot quickly as I set my mouth against the sting. She told me I was done and thanked me for coming, then left. There was no smiley face.

ABOUT THE AUTHOR

Drake Bennett attends Phillips Exeter Academy in his hometown of Exeter, New Hampshire. Soccer, lacrosse, "a lot of hiking, and the Grateful Dead" occupy much of his time, along with playing the violin.

It took a small boy to save him.

Seeking My Brother

by JULIE SMITH

The clear, strong voices of the monastic choir fill the air with their glorious song. I, Saul, am a holy man, and I sit by this river. Wide, deep, and slow, its beauty is overwhelming. I come here often—every day. Then I go back to the abbey to pray, eat, sing, and sleep. Sometimes I sleep by this river because I love this river. I learn from this river. I listen to it as I listen to my brothers singing their songs of devotion and sincerity. But I am both frightened and reassured by the predictable fate of this river. Later on in its course, my river will fall over the cataracts of time, then rush into the ocean of All and be mixed with everything.

Every day I must follow the river's example.

Before the blinding sun could flood the glorious landscape, which the abbey owns, I started walking to my river. I got only halfway to my destination when I saw, nestled in a gathering of dry leaves, a figure of starved and sunless proportions.

The child's head was tucked beneath the crease of its arm, asleep. I sat on a rock nearby, waiting for this child to awaken.

I looked far beyond what I could clearly see, and I knew the city was there. When I was still very young, I lived in the city with my family—until one autumn day when my brother and I were playing outside.

"Hey, you want to come climb this tree with me?"

I agreed, of course. Timothy was my older brother.

We ran to the tree. It was old and worn. Its branches stretched far from the trunk, as if to balance the unsteady mass.

"I'll go first."

I agreed.

Tim clambered up the side of the dark figure. Up and up. He made it to the top. I knew he would.

"Do you think I could climb up onto that branch over there?"

I nodded.

He inched his way out. Slowly, carefully. Every move was planned. Tim was so brave.

He was at the end of the branch. "YES! I knew I could do it."

So did I.

He was coming down, and then it would be my turn. But as he turned around, the tree branch snapped. I heard him scream. I ran to save him.

"TIM, TIM, TIM!" I yelled his name—forever.

My parents mourned his death. I'm sure they still do. I was the one still alive. So I was shunned.

Oh, how I missed him.

Mother and Father, if I can still call them that, sent

me to where I am now.

The sun slowly crept over the horizon. The chill of night disappeared under the warmth of the sun.

The figure stirred and rolled over. Before me was the face of a boy. I wasn't ready for what I saw: my brother's face was neatly woven into the boy's visage. The feelings that I felt, and still feel, for Timothy invaded my mind. The boy drowsily opened his eyes. They were not of my monastic brothers, but of the night and the stars.

"Hello, my child."

"Hello, sir," he replied.

"What are you called, son?"

"I am Chloe Patrick."

"I am Saul. Are you hungry?"

"Oh yes. I've been walking a long time!"

"Come with me."

I led him down the path that I've been walking almost all my life.

The holy building stood in all its simple grace. Even with its plain exterior, the beauty of this House of God was unmistakable. Gray pillars stood on either side of the entrance, protecting it.

I opened the majestic wooden door. Immediately, voices from deep inside exploded from the narrow doorway, filling the air with their beautiful melody. I led the peaceful boy into the vast kitchen.

As the boy was stuffing his mouth as politely as he could, I watched affectionately. Chloe finished eating and sat quietly.

I hadn't the faintest idea what he wanted me to do or say. So I waited for him to speak.

"I ran away from my orphanage. I was terrible there.

I was mean to everyone—even people I liked. I hate what they made me do. They never heard me. I couldn't stand it any longer. I won't go back. I'll run away again, I swear." His eyes were filled with tears and his face was deathly pale.

The tree branch snapped.

"What has happened to you to make you behave like this?"

There was no reply.

Quietly, I spoke to him. "I won't tell them that you are here. Where will you go?" He looked at me longingly, and I realized he wanted to go nowhere and that this could be the end of his journey.

"OK. You can stay here, son."

He smiled shyly. "Thank you."

The one day and one meal that I shared with Chloe turned to two days, then to a week, and soon it seemed that Chloe might stay for all days. During this time the runaway and I talked whenever possible. Our conversations usually focused on daily events, but one night the conversation turned to more serious matters.

We were talking of the river and how beautiful it stays all year round. Chloe said, "My brother would have adored this place, so peaceful and calm."

I questioned him about his brother. He stayed silent until he came to a decision. He concluded that he should tell me of his life.

"When I was young, I lived with my mother, father, and older brother, Dory. Not much older, only by a couple of years. Dory was old enough to know what was happening and understand it."

Chloe told me how his parents had got caught in a storm out in the middle of a lake. His father fell overboard and his mother jumped in after him. He pulled her under in his state of panic. Dory had to identify the bodies, being that the children were the only relatives. Dory changed drastically after the accident. They were sent to an orphanage until a home could be found for them. But Dory could not cope with all the changes that occurred so rapidly. Once he put a knife to his abdomen in hopes of escaping this world. The wardens of the orphanage found him just in time and he lived; but the doctors decided that he wasn't ready to go back. They sent him to an institution. Chloe found this out—and ran away.

There was silence after he finished telling me his story. I felt sympathy for Chloe, for I had also lost my brother. Only my brother was dead forever. I still feel the emptiness of my loss.

I sat with Chloe in my arms, not able to talk, for I was in as much pain as he was. We then fell into a deep sleep.

Morning came suddenly, and I realized I wanted Chloe to never leave.

I said, "Chloe, please—"

Chloe interrupted abruptly. "You have to help me go get Dory."

"I can't."

"I'm only a child; I need your help. You must!"

"I am a monk. I have vowed not to go into the city."

"I have a brother who doesn't know that he can be free."

"I have made a promise that I will always be faithful."

"Please! I need you. I must save my brother."

"I can't."

The next morning, Chloe and I walked down to the river. We followed it upstream. All was silent except for the rushing of the water.

Before dusk, we reached the outskirts of the city. Chloe stopped. He looked at me, sorrow and stars in his deep blue eyes.

"Please, Saul, I need you."

"I can't, Chloe. You will make it."

He turned and walked into the city lights and sounds. I watched until he had disappeared completely.

I still heard the river rushing along its winding path. Only now it was singing a new song—a song of love!

I will break my vows. Into the city I ran, seeking Chloe.

ABOUT THE AUTHOR

Julie Smith lives in Silt, Colorado, and attends Rifle High School in Rifle. Julie sews many of her own clothes, makes bead necklaces, and enjoys singing and New Age music. The idea for her story came from a dream she had.

He looked at me and said, "I so want to believe in my father, but the world has torn me apart."

My Grandfather's Shoes

by MATTHEW CHENEY

A few weeks ago I saw a movie about a French Resistance fighter during World War II, and it broke my heart because I remembered that summer and Jack and my grandfather's shoes.

I carry a picture of my grandfather in my wallet. He was a French Resistance fighter, but you could never tell from that grainy black-and-white photo. He doesn't look like a swashbuckling, machine gun-toting hero. He looks more like a man who spent most of his life in a library: wide-rimmed black glasses, high cheekbones with a thin layer of pale skin pulled over them, a receding hairline. My grandmother swore to the fact that he killed seventeen German soldiers and saved the lives of, in her words, "countless, countless citi-senz." He died in a concentration camp when he was thirty-three years old.

When I look at the picture, I remember the summer after either fifth or sixth grade, I don't remember which. Images and sounds and smells stumble up through my memory. I had made a new friend, a boy named Jack Wagner who had just moved into the neighborhood. Most people would pronounce his name wrong. He always had to say, "No, no, not Wagner. It's German. Vaaagner. Like the composer."

Jack Wagner. I carry a picture of him in my wallet, too. It's the only picture I ever saw of him, a picture my mother took the first week I knew him. The picture shows the two of us on our bicycles in my driveway. I cut Jack out of the picture and carry only him in my wallet; there is no reason for me to be there, too.

It really was a glorious summer. It resides in my mind like a Monet painting, or perhaps a Seurat. The suburban landscape was pastel-colored, the light refracted in such a way as to be almost blurred and almost impossibly clear. The houses sat in their small yards like bulldogs. The air smelled of freshly cut grass. Cars rumbled along the street, people talked to their neighbors over a hedge, the birds whistled, dogs barked, the wind rustled the branches of trees.

There was a massive maple tree at the end of our street, and I remember standing with Jack and admiring its foliage. The tree looked so tall and sturdy, so authoritative. My grandmother would say it looked "autocratic," since everything tall and sturdy and authoritative was, to her mind, "autocratic." She thought Boston was an autocratic city, full of autocratic skyscrapers and autocratic statues and autocratic bridges. I remember once she showed me a picture of my grandfather, looking as studious as ever, with the Eiffel Tower behind him. "Now doesn't that tower look autocratic?"

she said, as if it were the first time she had thought so. This summer the maple tree was especially autocratic, since its leaves had come early and completely hid its trunk.

There were blue skies almost every day, and I remember being amazed that the temperature stayed so constant and that there was always a slight breeze, as if the world were moving so fast the air couldn't stand still. The grass that summer was so green it seemed artificial.

I met Jack a week after the end of school. I was riding my bike down his street, a few blocks from my own. He had just moved in, and in the yard sat a couch and three ladder-back chairs. Jack was sitting on the couch, reading a book. I stopped my bike and asked, "Whatcha reading?"

He looked up shyly and closed the book. "Aw, just a book."

"What book?"

"Just a novel. It's by Beverly Cleary."

"Really? I love her books." I walked up to him. "You just move here?"

"Yeah. My parents had to go to town to get some stuff for lunch."

"They let you stay here alone?"

"Yeah."

"Wow," I said. "My parents don't do that much."

"Where do you live?"

"Coolidge Ave. Just a few blocks down. What's your name?"

"Jack. Jack Wagner."

I didn't see his parents that day. Jack took his bike out of the garage, and we went cruising through town.

For much of that summer we explored the area on our bicycles, establishing secret forts and paths to woods of fantasy.

One day the subject of our grandfathers came up. We were boasting about our fathers' achievements, when I decided that my grandfather was a far more color-ful figure than plain old Dad. We were in my house, and I told Jack that my grandfather had been a free-dom fighter in France and that he died in a concen-tration camp.

"No way," Jack said.

"Yes sir," I said. "Come here. I'll prove it."

I took him up into my parents' bedroom and showed him the shoes my grandfather had worn in the camp.

"Is it true?" Jack asked.

"Of course it's true," I said. Did he think me a liar?

"But it couldn't be," he said.

"Why not?"

"It never happened. My father says there were no concentration camps; there were no Jews or anybody killed. He says it's all a hoax by people who hate Ger-mans."

I was flabbergasted. No concentration camps? Was it possible? Anger rushed through me, but without di-rection. I was angry at Jack for proposing such a ridicu-lous idea, I was angry at my family for possibly lying to me, and I was angry at the world for not telling me there are different angles to every picture. I shook my head gently and tried to laugh the anger off. "That's silly," I said.

I have those shoes in front of me now. They are crude, with wooden soles and a canvas body so that they are as much like slippers as anything. There was only one size, and I have always thought that my grandfather's scholarly feet would be far too small to fit into such bulky, wide shoes. But they were his shoes.

That night at supper I told my parents what Jack had said. My parents were silent for a moment. They looked at each other as if a fear they had predicted but considered a phantom had suddenly taken shape in flesh and blood. My father coughed uncomfortably and asked, "Is this boy a friend?"

"Yes," I said quietly.

My father stared at his supper and shook his head slowly.

"Peter, you have to realize that your grandfather . . . your grandfather was a hero. He fought for a great cause, one of the greatest in history. Now, I don't want to preach to you, Peter, you are no longer a little boy, but I can't imagine what your grandfather would say if he were alive and he found out that his grandson was spending time with—" he coughed again and shuffled his food with his fork "—that type of . . . that type of person. This isn't a game."

I said quickly, "I know it's not a game and I don't—"

"Your father's right, dear," my mother said.

"But—"

My father looked at me. "I don't want you two to play together anymore."

"He sounds like a horrible child," my mother said.

"He's not—"

"Did you hear me?" my father asked.

"Yeah," I said.

My parents continued their conversation as if I wasn't there.

"His family's probably a pack of Nazis," my mother said. "His grandfather might have been an SS officer. That's probably why they left the country."

"Can you imagine? Can you imagine what blood must be on the hands of that family? My God, it's repulsive. Just to think that people like that exist, and in a good town like this. Just repulsive."

I wanted to protest, but my mother said, "Eat your peas."

I wasn't about to abandon Jack, of course. He quickly became my best friend. He and I didn't share many interests, but our personalities clicked. Often your best friends aren't the ones who think the same way you do, but the ones who are willing to disagree with you, the ones who see the world in different colors than you do.

Jack and I would play beneath a small bridge in the least residential area of town. The houses there were spread farther apart than at the center of town, and there were fields and clumps of old, withered trees. We biked out to that part of town and left our bikes in a wooded area in front of the bridge.

The bridge arched over a stream that was unusually low this summer, but still noticeably a stream. We jumped across the rocks, walked along the side of the bridge's smooth granite walls, and climbed some of the trees on the banks of the stream. We sat in the sand beneath the bridge and played cards, or a board game one of us brought, or threw pebbles into the water, or just talked. We were always afraid the old man who lived in the house past the bridge would come out and yell at us, but he never did. I doubt that he even knew we were there.

Occasionally Jack would come over to my house, or I would go over to his. He told me his parents had told him to stay away from me, that I wasn't the type of person he should hang around with, so we couldn't meet in either house very often. But if my parents or his parents had gone somewhere, we would gladly trade the sandy, wet haven of the bridge for the clean, dry comfort of a house.

From the horror stories my parents and grandmother had told me of Nazis, I expected to find the inside of Jack's home to be a dimly lit cavern, its walls covered with swastika flags and bookshelves displaying human skulls. Actually, it was a small cape with many windows, green carpet, and yellow walls. The walls were mostly bare, except for a print of Munch's *The Scream* and a small auburn tapestry in the living room. I only saw the interior of the house once, and only for a few minutes, but it so clashed with my preconception that I have never forgotten it.

Jack came over to my house twice. My parents always went shopping on Saturday afternoons and then went to a movie (they called it "our day out"). This was my first year of being left alone in the house without a babysitter.

One Tuesday my parents decided to take some time off from work and take a day trip to Vermont. My father was obsessed with Quechee Gorge, and he wanted to show it to my mother. I didn't want to go, and for some reason they let me stay home alone. I called Jack and told him to come over.

There was a knock at the door. I opened it. A tall,

silver-haired, leather-skinned man stood at the door. He seemed completely composed of right angles. He said, "Are you Peter Bisset?"

"Y-yes . . ." I said.

"I am Hermann Wagner. Jack's father."

I had expected him to have a German accent, but he spoke in precise English.

"Oh?"

"He tells me you have a pair of shoes that were worn in a concentration camp."

I nodded.

"I would like to see these shoes."

"I—my-my parents aren't home right now." Sweat grew from my palms.

"Surely they wouldn't mind if you just showed me the shoes."

"But—"

I didn't know what to do. I was terrified, yet it seemed to me that it would be impolite not to let this man in. He was a burly man, yet I sensed kindness within him. He had a warm smile and sparkling blue eyes. He held his massive hands in front of himself like a butler. I didn't think he would hurt me. Still, he was the son of a Nazi soldier and he didn't believe there had been any concentration camps. My grandmother had told me about the Nazis. "They smiled and made you comfortable. They were kind at first, but that was just a disguise so they could hurt you even more. You trusted them, and they shot you."

If I let him in the house, he might kill me. He might, but he only wanted to see the shoes. Why would he kill me? I hadn't done anything to him, unless he was angry that Jack and I had continued to be friends. But

I didn't think so. I trusted him, despite the warnings of my grandmother.

"Up-upstairs," I said quietly. I led him upstairs and into my parents' room. I opened the closet and pulled out the cardboard box holding the shoes. I opened the box and he looked inside.

He stared at the shoes. His left cheek twitched. He ran his tongue along his lips and whispered something inaudible. Tears slowly washed across his eyes. He ran his hand along the shoes as if he was touching Christ's crown of thorns. He breathed rapidly and seemed to groan. He whispered, "*Es tut mir leid, Vater. Es tut mir leid.*" Slowly, he put the shoes back into the box which I held. He looked at me, tears sliding down his cheeks. "I want to believe . . . I so want to believe in my father, but the world has torn me apart." He turned and walked back downstairs and out the door.

That night at dinner my parents talked about Quechee Gorge and Vermont. They wondered if we should move there. "I saw Jack today," I said, interrupting their discussion of farmers, cows, and manure.

Silence. My father's fork clanged against his plate. "I thought I told you not to see him."

"He came over. I told him to leave, but he only stayed for a minute."

"What did he want?" my mother asked.

"He—" I didn't know what to say. I hadn't thought out my lie. "He wanted to say he was sorry."

"For what?"

"For not believing. He said he was sorry he hadn't believed in my grandfather, and he . . . he thanked me for showing him the shoes."

My parents didn't say anything. They both finished

their supper, muttered something about Vermont, and then my mother told me to put the dishes in the dishwasher.

I didn't see Jack after that. I called him once or twice, but he always said he was busy that day. He said he was busy every day. He transferred to a school across town, miles away from the one I attended. Occasionally I would ride my bike past his house, but I never saw him.

Two days ago my mother sent me my grandfather's shoes. She pulled them out of the closet as she prepared to move into an apartment. My father died a year ago and she doesn't need the big house anymore. She sent them to me with a letter saying they would just take up space in her apartment, and that they had always seemed to fascinate me, so why didn't I take them. She told me that if I didn't want them, I might as well throw them away.

I don't think I'll throw them away. I think I'll keep them here, on my desk. Whenever I am unhappy, I can look at the shoes and think about the misery my grandfather must have suffered. Whenever I don't want to fight the cruelties of the world, but ignore them like junk mail, I will look at these shoes and think of Jack and his father. No, I won't throw them away.

ABOUT THE AUTHOR

Matthew Cheney lives in Plymouth, New Hampshire, and attends The New Hampton School in New Hampton. His main interest, he reports, is writing: "Reading is fun, too—especially the works of Philip K. Dick, John Irving, Franz Kafka, and Calder Willingham." He reports that he has just completed his first novel and plans to paper his bathroom with rejection slips.

She believed in its protection . . .

Moonshine

by JENNIFER MCLUNE

Lula's hair was thick and nappy like that old dusty picture on the mantel that showed her auntie before the hot comb was invented. Jet black and full of kinks that she'd run her fingers through and release secret smells that her momma mistook for funk. But she and Bessie knew better. They'd sit mesmerized for hours in the forest and release that smell and feel it go waltzing slowly along with the pine. No one knew but them that Jesus' mother was a black woman who didn't press her hair. So, lying there among the pines and forest whispers, they felt blessed.

"Bessie, you reckon we's doin' right?" Lula asked.

"What you mean?"

"I mean runnin' away from church and all. Momma'll have a fit if she catch us."

"You scared of gettin' a whoppin'?" Bessie asked.

"Sure, ain't you?"

"No, ma'am. I'd take a thousand whoppin's 'fore

I let them touch my hair," she said. "Don't you know those red-hot teeth burns hotter than a switch?"

"It's just that I'm scared. Bessie, I ain't as strong as you yet."

"It ain't got nothin' to do with strength, Lula. It's faith you need. Faith in something. *Anything,* just so long as you know it's yours."

Lula said, "I ain't got no faith, neither. Momma got all the faith."

"No, Momma got all her faith in a white god. And she put all her strength in Seaboy, a man who smell worse than a whiskey barrel and make us call him Daddy." Bessie took a long breath and drew in the mellow smell of the pine, ran her long, thin fingers through her hair, and began to braid and cry. "Faith, Lula, ain't like land. The white man can't own it. Seaboy and Momma can't, neither. It's ours."

Lula looked at her sister, tried to look into her. Bessie was a rock. A blue-black stone. She herself should be the one crying, not Bessie.

"Don't cry, Bessie. We's gonna be all right!" she said, but her words got carried away into the far-off ears of corn.

Bessie continued, "Faith's the stuff you believe in. It's the lifeblood of all us black women. What you believe in, Lula?"

"Nothin', I guess," Lula said.

"Oh, come on—there's gotta be sumpthin'," Bessie said. "Forget all that hocus-pocus church folks been feedin' you and tell me what you believe in."

For a moment Lula melted, a droplet of black dew into the soil. No one had ever asked her what she believed in. She had always known deep inside, but knew she had to keep it secret. Ways that weren't Momma's ways were there inside her. Her Jesus wasn't Momma's Jesus, but her Jesus shone just as bright. She knew things, felt things, that she was sure would make her momma cry. So, real young, she learned the cover of silence. She learned that things inside are best kept there. At times, though, she wished she could be as wild as Bessie, always talking to grown folks like they were young, and always asking questions. Whenever she tried being wild like that, she only tripped over her own feet. She was just a clumsy jerk, she thought.

But then again, she was *there*, lying in a pine forest with her sister while the rest of their family was singing praises at church. Lord, was she a demon! She knew Momma was probably praying and shouting for her right now. She was always praying. Bessie always said that was her main problem. She said what's the point of praying to a white god when the white man ain't doing nothing for us right here.

Lula prayed too. She prayed hard. On her knees by her bedside, trying so hard to picture Jesus the way he looked on the cover of the Sunday school bulletin— a golden-haired white man in a white robe, holding a white lamb in his arms. She tried to pour her sins and needs and wants at his feet, tried to look into those blue eyes and find something to save her. But afterwards she never really felt forgiven, only pardoned. She wondered if she could get to heaven on pardoned sins. Momma said that to get there you had to be a born-again Christian. She said you had to be baptized by the spirit and given back to the world anew. Lula didn't know about all that, but as soon as she came back to herself and let the forest wrap around her again, she felt new. Born again.

"I believe," Lula said, "in the moon. Because she's big and white and full, like a pregnant lady in the sky. And when she ready to nurse the planets which are her babies, it rains. She got magical powers Jesus ain't figured out yet." Lula stopped. She was going to hell for sure now. But Bessie's eyes urged her on. "It sort of like," she continued, "like them miracles can't nobody explain. Like when Seaboy's crops be dryin' up and nothin' won't grow. And we all be hungry and the white folks buggin' Momma for the rent. And all of a sudden, when things can't get much worse, and Momma's knees be sore from prayin' so hard, it rains."

"That's *her* who does it?" Bessie asked. For the first time it was Lula who had the answers.

"Yep," said Lula. "Only God gets the credit."

"Do you know that there's people that want to own her?"

"Who? The Pregnant White Lady in the Sky?"

"Yep," Bessie said.

"White folks?"

"Of course. Who else want to own the moon? They been stickin' flags in her with names sayin' *this here's mine*. Down at the barber shop Miss Addie put on the radio, and all you hear is about white folks goin' to the moon," said Bessie.

"But there's some things you can't never own," Lula said, confused. "The moon ain't nobody's. I don't care how many flags you got. I mean, it don't matter what your color is, how much money you got, or where you live. You look up and there she is. The Pregnant White Lady in the Sky. And her milk drop down on all of us."

"Well, Lula, there's things bigger than us. They's called countries. And I read that they take what they want with iron and blood. They want to chop up the moon and sell her parts—a leg for France, an arm for England, and her big belly for the U.S."

"How 'bout Africa? Ain't there none left for her?" asked Lula.

"Nope, 'cause she already been there."

Just then, the Pregnant White Lady in the Sky began to nurse. The girls ran barefoot through the pine, the broad arms of trees protecting them from the rain. It fell fiercely like needles on their backs once they reached the roadside. But they just walked slowly home to a warm fire and a hot switch.

ABOUT THE AUTHOR

Jennifer McLune lives in Manhasset, New York, where she attends Manhasset High School. She has been a contributing editor for her school's literary magazine and is presently an exchange student in Brazil. "I spend most of my time writing," she reports. "My work is so personal that it seems strange that anyone would want to read it but me." Listening to jazz and reading are other favorite pastimes.

The gods made him immortal.

Theron

by ELLEN PERRY

There once was a time, before the great heroes were alive, years before the Argonauts went on the perilous Quest for the Golden Fleece, when the mighty god Zeus became disappointed at the wickedness of all the people on Earth and decided to punish them. He and his brother Poseidon, the powerful God of the Sea, plotted together to send a terrible flood to destroy mankind, but Artemis intervened. She believed that if one man could be created flawless beyond compare by the divinities, he, as king, would reform the Earth people.

A vast meeting was held on Mt. Olympus. The great and lesser gods participated, as did the gods of Earth. They discussed at length the proposition made by Artemis. Though some were a bit skeptical, the majority of the gods decided that trying it would be better than simply bringing disaster to the land all at once.

Plans took shape immediately to begin the creation

of one supreme mortal who would bring peace and good will to the people of Earth. Many of the divinities agreed that blessing the man with their own individual best traits and talents would give him many admirable characteristics. Hephaestus, God of Fire, was asked to design the face and body of the man, and he cast and shaped him from bronze. He worked painstakingly for days. When he finally finished, the blacksmith god was pleased with his endeavors; the man was beautiful, his features made perfect by flame.

Theron, as the man was named by Hestia, was brought to Mt. Olympus at once. He lay before Zeus, motionless and very handsome, on a slab of bronze. Once again, the divinities were brought together, with the exception of two. Apollo, God of Light, Music, and Poetry, was envious of the stately mortal and had no desire to contribute any of his own gifts to him. Ares, however, the murderous, cruel God of War, had been commanded by Zeus and Hera to keep away during the fashioning of the king. They and the other gods believed he had nothing worth granting Theron, which was true: he was violent and full of hatred.

Touching the statue's forehead, Athena began the ritual by instilling in Theron her gifts of wisdom, reason, and understanding. Hermes joined her, presenting Theron with his unique craftiness and wit. Artemis touched his strong arms and hands, and he was blessed with the art of the hunt. Finally, by placing her delicate hand on Theron's lifeless chest, Aphrodite warmed his cold heart and gave him a sense of love and compassion.

Zeus, who had been watching all this time from his throne, rose to his feet; the gods drew back in awe, nearly blinded by his radiance. With all the power he could muster from his mind and body, Zeus hurled a thunderbolt deep into the statue, shattering it into a shower of sparks and fire. When the smoke cleared and a colorful mist rose, Theron appeared. His eyes were a deep brown, and his hair lay in curls about his head. He was alive, the perfect mortal, a king who possessed traits of the gods themselves. Theron was a masterpiece.

The Graces fell in love with him instantly. They sacrificed themselves so that their spirits, Splendor, Mirth, and Good Cheer, would enter Theron's spirit and belong to him. Thus, he was not only a wise and skilled king, but also a loving, merry man who would teach and inspire the people of Earth. The divinities rejoiced!

What the gods did not know, however, was that Eris, the Goddess of Discord, who would later cause trouble with Paris just before the Trojan War, and Ares were scheming together. Eris devised a plan, which Ares carried out months later at a banquet in King Theron's palace.

Before the feast, while the guests were dancing merrily and the crowded ballroom was buzzing with talk and laughter, Ares crept silently into the dining hall. He placed a powerful sleeping potion, which would take effect within hours, in Theron's wine.

Some time after the grand reception, Theron found himself growing drowsy, just as Ares had intended. The king staggered into his chambers and fell into a deep, dreamless sleep. There, waiting in the shadows, stood the evil war god. Ares cut himself with a silver blade and then made a small incision in Theron's chest.

He watched as his own vile blood trickled into Theron's tiny wound. Ares sneered with satisfaction, cackling at the "gift" he had given to the king. This impeccable being now had a merciless, violent temper, and though it was only a fraction of his composition, still it was there, coursing through his veins, and would always be part of him.

Time passed, and mankind continued to improve under the rule of King Theron, companion of the Olympians. Poseidon presented him with a beautiful stallion. Even Apollo came to appreciate him. The two became great friends, and, although he had been selfish and jealous before, Apollo taught Theron to play the lyre.

But Theron was closest to Artemis and was with her more than almost any other. He knew she was responsible for giving him life. She, the Goddess of the Moon, admitted to him that she was lonely in the sky at night, so Theron kept her company every time the sun disappeared by talking with her as he rested on the Earth. But still she was sad, for as she looked down upon him from her perch in the night sky, he seemed so far away.

For several years mankind prospered; everything was going according to plan. Food was plentiful, and men were generous and kind to one another. For the first time in decades, there was peace in the land. But then one day, as ominous storms brewed in the skies and thunder rolled like waves across heavy dark clouds, King Theron flew into a fit of rage over a minor conflict with a peasant and killed twenty innocent men with the blade of his sword.

The land became chaotic and immediately returned to its wicked ways. Those who at one time had faith in their king now scorned him and put on their old masks of bitter hatred and suspicion. Evil plagued the land; people cursed and even killed each other, as if to find answers to their hurting hearts' questions. Silently, Ares congratulated himself.

Theron was haunted by his conscience day and night, overcome with guilt and remorse. Deeply grieved, he locked himself in the cellar of his palace without food for many days, trying to reason with himself. He couldn't understand why he had betrayed the gods who had given him life and the people who had trusted and admired him. Finally, one dark night, he decided that he was not deserving of the life given him; with the sword that had killed so many others, he stabbed himself in the chest.

As King Theron lay dying alone in the seclusion of his damp cellar, he whispered a final wish. "Please," he called to the gods, "pity me and allow me to spend eternity with the one merciful enough to give the world a second chance. I want to comfort and love her, the lonely Goddess of the Moon, as she shines in the cold night sky."

And with these words, he died.

The Graces, who had perished to give Theron their souls, returned to life as the blood, both good and evil, spilled from his broken heart. They wept over his tranquil, beautiful body, then fled to Mt. Olympus to tell Zeus about Ares, for they had been a part of Theron and were the only ones to know the truth. The heartless, vicious god was severely punished for the heinous deed he had committed.

The Olympians mourned the loss of King Theron. Artemis in particular suffered from a heavy, anguished heart. Upon seeing her rare tears, Zeus was profoundly moved and possessed of a divine inspiration: "May the mortal king live forever in the realm of my sky near the one who loved him most!" And with these words the night burst into color, as it had the day Theron was brought to life. Sparks and flame and glittering brilliance illuminated the emptiness of the night. Theron's spirit and lifeless form were taken from the Underworld and transformed by Zeus into a million tiny shards of sparkling light. To the delight of Artemis, they were scattered like diamonds everywhere across the velvet sky.

Today, when night falls and lonely dreamers stare into space to wonder about the miracles of the universe, they sense that the moon and stars are enchanted with each other, that they laugh and talk in their own secret language until the sunlight frightens them away. They shine together on the world below to give inspiration and hope to those who will listen to their midnight love songs. Though the light of morning dims their silver radiance, the stars and moon will not be parted, and will shine together till the end of time.

About the Author

Ellen Perry lives in Asheville, North Carolina, and attends North Buncombe High School in Weaverville. Her interests include playing the clarinet, running track, and involvement in Student Council and SADD.

Does a rainbow cast a shadow?

The Chosen One

by KIMBERLY NORTHRIP

The sunshine poured through the windows. It danced over the curves in the furniture and dripped down onto the carpet, where it pooled and remained. My cat floated dreamily in one of those pools. She's an Egyptian Mau, and when she lies in the sunshine, her hair gleams like melted bronze. I was watching her from my bed.

Our house is set up strangely; I have one giant room that serves as a sitting room/bedroom, and a little kitchen-thing with a sink and a tiny refrigerator. Then, if you go down the hall, you find another bedroom (the real one, actually) that I use as a study, and a connecting bath. On the opposite side of the hall are the stairs—one flight climbing up to the roof, the other down to my parents' rooms, which are totally different from mine.

Actually, I should say my dad's rooms, because my mom hasn't lived with us for twelve years. She just took off one day while I was at my babysitter's house. She didn't even tell us she was going to go; she was just gone when my dad and I got home. My dad says my mom was always flighty. I don't know; I don't really remember much about her. He also says my sister is just like her.

My sister's name is Arden. Neither of us is really sure about her. But at least we know where she is. Arden loves to skip around the world. Last year she studied in Paris; then she went to some tiny village in Africa to do charity work. China came next, after that India. She's in Canada now, somewhere up north. Arden never has been one to let the grass grow under her feet. Dad says she's just like Mom. That explains it.

Right now I'm sitting up in bed, thinking all this. My knees are tucked up against my chest with my arms wrapped around them, holding them in place, and my chin is resting on them. This is my favorite position for thinking. Arden says I close up just like a clam when I'm thinking. Arden thinks like a bird; she just flits from one thought to the next. I don't really know why I'm thinking all this. Maybe it's because of the phone call. My dad answered the first time the phone rang. He said whoever it was had just hung up. It rang again last night, after Dad went out. I answered. A woman's voice asked hesitantly, "Is this Arden?"

"No," I said, a little annoyed. Arden is barely here anymore; I thought everyone knew that.

"Then this must be Allison," she said, and then she started crying and hung up.

I know who called, both those times. It was my mother. I don't know why she has decided to step back into our lives now, but apparently she has. I'm not really sure what to do. I don't know if I'm going to tell my dad or not. He doesn't really talk about my mom much. I was small when she left; I don't remember all that much about her. I remember that she always smelled clean, like soap and water and toothpaste. And I remember her laugh. It would dance and swoop through the air; it always made me laugh when I heard it. And she loved me.

I know it doesn't sound like she loved me, because she left, but I know she really did. I can remember that much. I suppose she must have stopped loving my dad. Or maybe she never loved him at all. I know that when my dad tells Arden, "You're just like your mother," it's not really a compliment. I suppose you could even say my dad hates her, if it's possible for my dad to really hate anyone at all. But I guess he does hate her, in his own way. I don't think I'll tell him she called.

Arden is coming home tomorrow. She said she can't live in Canada anymore. "There's no sunshine here, Turtle. How can you have life where there's no sunshine?" Arden always calls me Turtle. She says it's because I'm so slow and thoughtful. When I remind her that the slow turtle beat the hare, she just laughs.

Daddy and I are going to the airport to pick her up. She's coming in very late, which means night driving. I love driving in the dark with my dad. We never talk, just sit together and think. That's the way it always is with my dad. There are no uncomfortable silences that must be filled with idle chatter when my dad and I are alone together. When Arden is home, everything always seems a little louder; the world just seems to move a little faster. Just the thought of Arden coming seems to make things speed up. Ever since she called this morning to tell us she was coming home tonight, my father has been rushing around madly, cleaning the house, making sure Arden's room is all ready, and stocking the cupboard with all her favorite foods. He always gets so excited before Arden comes home.

I remember the day before she came home after being gone the first time. Not only did he clean the house, he also baked a cake, and he made a huge sign which read, "Welcome Home, Arden!" He blew up balloons and put streamers all over the house. I guess that's why it upset him so much when she told him she was only stopping over for about two hours on her way to Africa. But that's just like Arden—you never can tell if she's coming or going.

Arden's been home a week now. Poor Daddy, he never knows quite what to do when she's here. She's his favorite daughter, but that's just because she's so Arden. Having Arden in the house is like having your own private rainbow flitting around. She completely befuddles Daddy; he never knows what to expect or think of Arden. That's why he likes me. He always understands me because we're alike. But Arden is just like my mom, and she's one person my dad never understood.

We got another call last night. Arden and I were sitting on the couch, eating popcorn and watching the late show while we waited for Dad to come back with the movie, when the phone rang. Arden answered this time. I could only hear one side of the conversation. "Hello," Arden said. "Yes, this is she. Who's this?

Who . . . What did you say? Oh, oh my. Where are
you? Yes, yes. Tomorrow. Yes, she'll come. OK," and
then she hung up. She looked at me. "Turtle, do you
know who that was?"

I nodded. "When do we have to meet her?" I asked
softly.

We left at 4:30 the next day. Dad was working late,
so there were no explanations. We went to the park
across town. It was cold out, with the sun gleaming
like crystallized ice through the trees. It had rained,
and everywhere I looked water glistened. Arden had
been very quiet the whole drive over.

I wonder what she thought when Mom left. She
had been almost twelve. Arden never talked about
Mom leaving, which is strange because she talks about
everything else. It must have really hurt her. She must
hate Mom, too. I never really thought about Arden
hating anybody. But I could tell from the way she
gripped the steering wheel and was quiet that she really did. But she still loved her, too. I could see that
in her eyes.

We parked over on the west side of the park. I
looked around at all the other cars parked over there,
trying to guess which one was my mother's. One Mercedes was parked shyly next to a Volkswagen bug and
an ancient Ford. It seemed to fit what I remembered
of my mother. Elegance seemed her due; I remembered the way her laugh would splash through the air.
Yes, the Mercedes.

We walked directly to the fountain in the center of
the park. It was on, and the water spouted into the air
joyously, making rainbows in the sky. I tried to conjure up an image of my mother. She had the same eyes

as my sister, I knew that. Arden and I both have blue eyes, but hers are clear, pure cornflower blue, while mine are a steely navy color. My mother would have blond hair, too, just like Arden's. My own hair is dark brown. Arden has golden skin and flushed cheeks, so that means my mother probably has golden skin and flushed cheeks. In short, I should be looking for an older Arden.

Just then a woman walked up to us. "Arden?" she asked. When Arden nodded, she looked at me and said, "You must be Allison." I nodded too, trying to figure out who this woman was. "I'm your mother," she said then. "I've missed you both so much."

I stared. This woman couldn't be my mother. She didn't look anything like Arden. Oh, her eyes were that cornflower blue, but they were empty and dead, whereas Arden's glimmered with light and life. Her hair was blond, like Arden's, and cut in the same sort of style. But Arden's hair danced and sparkled like stray sunbeams, while her hair was dull and limp, almost colorless. Her skin was sallow and yellow; Arden's was golden and crisp. It was as if Arden was alive, while this woman had long been dead.

"I know this seems strange, meeting me like this. But I've been wondering about you girls for twelve years now. I just didn't know what to, or how to . . ." She bumbled to a stop, scared and uncertain. We stood around, the silence growing stiffer and more tense with each passing breath.

Finally, Arden said, so softly I almost missed it, "What happened to you, Mom?"

The woman's eyes filled with tears. "I don't know," she gasped, trying to catch her breath. "I don't know anymore."

She sat down hard on the edge of the fountain. She fumbled with the catch on her purse and pulled out a pack of cigarettes. She lit one and inhaled deeply with relief, her hands shaking so badly the ash scattered like tears over the ground. Arden turned and walked away.

I stood there for a while, listening to her breathe. I watched her puff away the cigarette, then light up another one. The flame bounced off the wedding band she wore. "Did you remarry?" I asked politely.

She shook her head. "I could never leave you girls," she said, without looking at me. I stared at her incredulously. I backed away from her, shaking my head and laughing. Who did she think she was fooling? I turned and walked back to the car, without looking back.

Two weeks passed quickly. Neither Arden nor I had forgotten the meeting with our mother, but it quickly melted into one of those trivial incidents that you never think of, but at the same time you never quite forget. We were going on with our lives when the police called. They said our mother had killed herself. She had drunk herself into a stupor and then slit her wrists. I knew I hadn't smelled soap on her in the park. Arden and I were the only two people at her funeral, aside from one man. He had long, dark hair and brooding, bloodshot eyes. He stood by her grave and wept like a child. "Stupid drunk," Arden hissed bitterly. Then she turned and walked away. I stayed, staring up at the casket.

The sun slipped behind a cloud then, and the world turned gray. I closed my eyes and tried to conjure up an image of the mother I once had, but all that came to my mind was the way she had looked at the funeral home, lying so still and cold in the casket. I searched my soul for something; I knew something had to be there. This woman was my mother, after all. I opened my eyes and reached up to wipe away the tears that I knew wouldn't be there. I had no tears for this woman, this woman who could have been my mother. I turned and started to walk away, but stopped after going only a little way. I looked back. Her coffin was spilling over with dark red roses. I remembered Arden telling me, long ago, that roses were my mother's favorite flowers. I walked slowly back to the coffin and stroked the soft, scented flowers on the top. I pulled until one came free from the others. It was a perfect rose, deep in color and heavily scented. I slipped it into my pocket and hurried away.

We never told our father that our mother had died. We never told him Arden and I went to the funeral. I thought about telling him several times, but I always stopped myself. It would be a waste of time to tell him. I think Mom died for him a long time ago.

It's been two years since that day. Arden is still living with us; she never left after our mother died. I'm supposed to be a lot older now; it has been two years. But I'm not. Arden has aged, though. To look at her you'd think it'd been a dozen years instead of just two. I'm sitting on my bed the same way I sat the day after my mother called, with my knees tucked up and my arms around them, my head on my knees. My cat is still floating in a pool of sunshine on the floor. My dad is at work, and Arden is lying dead in the bathroom.

She killed herself this morning. I knew she would. I've been waiting for it, I suppose. Every day she looked a little bit more like our mother. That's how I knew it was coming. First it was her skin. It lost the glow. Then her hair went dull and lackluster. And I began to smell it on her in the morning, the combination of stale smoke and alcohol. Then her eyes lost their light, their animation. And I knew it was coming, coming like the tide. And I knew that nothing I said or did would change the fact.

She did it this morning. I heard her crashing around. She was drunk, I suppose. But not like the normal word-slurring, sloppy drunk. More calm and wise. More like she had drugged herself to drown the panic. I watched her from the hallway, standing just outside the bathroom door. I don't think she saw me; it didn't make a difference if she did. She took almost a whole bottle of sleeping pills, one by one. A part of me was tempted to run into the bathroom, grab the bottle, and fling it to the floor. The pills would scatter everywhere, crashing loudly on the hard tile floor. And then a voice inside me asked, *Why? Why should I stop her? There's nothing left for her here, and she has nowhere left to go. Why should I stop her? It's none of my business anyway.* But I could not force myself to turn away, and so I stood there, watching, as she stared into the mirror blindly. She turned suddenly. She walked over to the door, shut it, then locked it. I heard the water run in the sink, imagined I heard the slicing of flesh. She made no sound as she died, or if she did, it was drowned out by the swirling water.

I'm sitting on my bed trying to decide what to do. I know I should call the police. I will sometime. I'm

not really sad she's dead. I don't think I ever really
knew Arden. She was more like a wild thing kept in a
cage than a sister, a person of flesh and blood. But if
you cage a wild thing, you kill its spirit. And then it
will die, too. We caged her spirit, my dad and I did,
with our simple, everyday way of living life. We bound
her to us, and she could not escape. So I suppose we
killed her. It's like my mother. Even after she was gone,
we still kept her soul in our cage. She tried to break
free and run, but it didn't work. My sister saw she
couldn't run anymore, either. I bowed my head and
cried then. I don't know why—it just seemed like the
right time. I rose and went to the mirror. I searched
and searched, but there were no traces of my mother
or of Arden there. I went to the phone and called the
police.

I don't remember exactly what I said to them, only
that they assured me they would come right away. The
operator's voice soothed me; it sounded so strong and
competent, as if even a tragedy of this sort could be
easily met and dealt with. I hung up the phone feeling stronger somehow. My fingers traced my father's
phone number almost of their own volition. The
phone rang again and again, the dull buzzing numb-
ing my senses and thoughts until only one was clear,
that he must not be in his office, that I should call
again later . . . The receiver was just slipping from my
grasp when I heard his familiar "Hello?"

"Daddy, please come home," I said, staring down
at my fingers twisting and twirling the telephone cord.
I could hear him hesitate.

"Allison, dear, I'm kind of busy now . . ."

"Daddy, please," I replied, so softly that the shaking of my voice was almost inaudible.

"I'm on my way." I heard him say Arden's name as I replaced the receiver.

The first thing my father saw when he stepped into the hall was the rapidly spreading pool of water on the floor in front of the bathroom. Just inside the door, a tight knot of people murmured confidences to one another. Perhaps he even saw the violent red streaks on the sink and the tile, already turning into ugly brown stains. Then he saw me. "Allison, what's happening?" he asked as he came toward me. I met his eyes then, and he stopped suddenly, recoiling almost as if I had hit him in the stomach. "Oh, dear God— Arden!"

I could feel his tears on my shoulder and thought, ironically, that it was he who should be comforting me. He always had before. But it didn't really matter to me anymore; I was OK now. Maybe we would even be happier now, without the shadows Arden and my mother had thrown over us.

ABOUT THE AUTHOR

Kimberly Northrip attends Carroll High School in her hometown of Southlake, Texas. In addition to reading and spending time with her friends and family, Kimberly enjoys hockey, basketball, and playing with her cat, Bandit. She has been a section editor of her school yearbook for the past several years and is a member of the National Honor Society, the International Club, and Academic Decathlon.

Shedding the boredom of summer . . .

Night Heat

by MIKE LEWIS

About 11 P.M. I decided to cruise. It was a Saturday night, a while past sundown. I'd been at home all day and there wasn't anything cool on TV. Nobody else was there. That was OK; I didn't feel like talking much anyway. I was in a state of supreme boredom, and when it's this bad, there aren't too many things that can get you going.

I was watching a Mexican TV station. My Spanish was getting better, and the news reporter was extremely good-looking, but I still couldn't understand more than a few words of what she said. I finally gave up and hit the power. I grabbed my skateboard and Copilot mug and left. Once on the street, I headed for an old buddy's pad.

It was a warm night, not really hot, but the humidity was enough to raise some sweat on my brow. I could feel the heat rising from the pavement. There were a few moths circling the lamp out by the gas pumps. An occasional car went down the street. At Stop 'n' Go at 11:30 P.M., not much ever happens.

". . . so anyway," Jimmy rambled on, "my dad is wasted out of his mind, cruisin' down the highway. I mean, this guy is all over the road. Sooner or later, some cop pulls us over and asks him if he's been drinkin'. First word that comes out of his mouth: 'No.' See, it was the only thing he could say without slurrin'."

John Cannon, Jimmy Newton, and I were all sitting against one of the walls outside the store, pretty much waiting for something to happen, which it probably wouldn't. I was getting bored listening to Jimmy rag on his dead dad, so I decided to cruise. I grabbed my Copilot mug and skateboard and pulled myself to my feet.

"Dudes, I gotta be cruisin'. Catch you later, John."

"Aw, come on, Mikeeeey," John said, half-tauntingly. "Why you gotta go so soon?"

"I dunno, man," I said with a dull kind of voice. "I'm gonna get a Coke refill and skate around for a while."

"Whatever, man. Mañana."

"Yeah . . ."

I pushed open the door and walked in. The air conditioner was running, and I was met with a refreshing blast of arctic air. I looked over to the register. Oh boy, my favorite person in the whole world was on duty tonight: Bill. Bill looks like a cross between Dr. Red Duke and a Texas Highway Patrol officer. He's tall, thin, wears wire frame glasses, and could always use another shave. About forty, I'd say.

I think Bill has some kind of paranoia about kids, or maybe just about me, because whenever I'm in the store he won't take his eyes off me. He thinks I'm some kind of thief. I hate his attitude, mostly because I can't remember the last time I stole something. Stealing is lazy, and I happen to be a Boy Scout. Not that the title carries much weight these days.

"Ah, Bill," I greeted him. "I suppose you want to know what I plan to rip off tonight."

"Very funny."

I took my mug over to the soda machine, put some ice in it, and filled it to the brim with life-giving Coca-Cola. I slapped the cap on the top and walked back to the counter. I dug into my pocket, got out three quarters, and deliberately dropped each one onto the counter, letting it spin around when it hit. It had the intended effect of annoying Bill, and I was happy.

"I tell ya, man," I said, "the only person who gets ripped off around here is the customer."

He didn't say anything, just dropped a dime and a penny into my hand. I went out the door, back into the heat. John and Jimmy were still out there, waiting for the world to end or their cigarettes to run out, whichever came first. Both would probably have the same effect on them.

"Hey, Mikey," said John, "loan me a quarter for stogs, wouldja?"

"Right . . ." I said. I'd been trying forever to get him to quit smoking.

I dropped my board on the concrete and started skating down the sidewalk beside the Quadrangle Mall, which Bill's store is a part of. There weren't any lights in the parking lot, and the stars shone brightly. A minute later I got to the end of the sidewalk and dropped off onto the pavement. I glanced back to see

John and Jimmy skate off into the darkness, probably heading for John's place. I turned back around and kept skating down the inclined parking lot, sipping my ice-cold Coke.

At the entrance I turned out of the lot and onto the street itself, just as a car ripped by out of nowhere, blasting heavy metal. The car passed me and tore down the street, away from the loop, doing well over a hundred. After it was gone, I started skating south on Broadway, toward Loop 410.

I was feeling energetic. There wasn't a car in sight, and the street was mine. The pavement was smooth, and my board seemed to glide. I had five lanes to move in. I felt a warm wind blow over my face. I skated beside the airport property, with the landing lights blinking in the distance like stars flickering on the horizon. There couldn't have been a soul for a mile around. I felt awake, able to take in all my surroundings at once. It was like I was meditating as I skated, and the feeling was exhilarating.

This must be what they mean when they say you have to feel the night. Anybody who hasn't wouldn't understand.

I got to Jim's Diner on the other side of Loop 410 about twenty minutes and two miles later, racing my shadow all the way. I would pass it as I approached each streetlamp; then it would leap in front as I passed them. I walked into the diner, used the john, and walked back out and started skating to my house, not even stopping for breath.

I made the trip back even faster, about fifteen minutes. By then it was about midnight. Just as I was skating across the Stop 'n' Go parking lot, my Rocky Mountain

High gave out and I got a massive nap attack. My house was in sight from the lot, but, after short deliberation, I decided to spend the night at John's, which wasn't too far away.

Five minutes later I was at his door. Nobody else was home and John had forgotten to lock the back door, so I let myself in. I opened his door and entered the lair. His room looked as it always had, Motley Crue and Metallica posters on the walls, clothes and junk piled on the floor two feet deep, cracked mirror, a huge waterbed that took up half the room, and a faint smell of refried beans. He was playing his Nintendo, and I guessed Jimmy must have gone home. I muttered a sleepy greeting and flopped down on the waterbed.

"Hey, Mike, didn't expect to see you by here. Hey, man, about tomorrow . . ."

I was out cold before he could finish the sentence.

So ended another night in San Antonio, Texas, summer of 1990.

That night I dreamt I met the Mexican news reporter, and my Spanish had much improved for the occasion.

ABOUT THE AUTHOR

Mike Lewis lives in San Antonio, Texas, where he attends Douglas MacArthur High School. He reports that his interests are "skating (boards), Boy Scouts, computers, martial arts, weapons, choir, eating, sleeping, and going to school."

How to snag Mr. Right.

The Valiant Princess

by HEATHER GARRETT

Once upon a time a Valiant Princess was searching for a Meek and Gentle Prince, for she had been taught that if a prince and princess are to marry, one should be strong and courageous, while the other should be timid and meek. No one could deny that the princess was strong and courageous, but there seemed to be a distressing lack of Meek and Timid Princes.

Not that the lack had ever bothered her before. She had spent most of her time roughhousing with the local princes, and left the meekness to her mother.

Just lately, however, her father had started insisting that she marry soon. He said he wanted her to settle down for her own sake, but the princess rather suspected it had more to do with the complaints he had been receiving about her from nearby kingdoms. They claimed, with justification, that the Valiant Princess had been killing off all their best dragons, and leaving the princesses that they guarded without any Heroic Princes to marry. It was all very annoying, they said, and ought to be stopped.

The problem, of course, was where to find such a husband. All the neighborhood princes came eagerly to woo her. Unfortunately, however, they all left just as quickly as they'd come when the princess started asking questions like, "How good are you at fancy embroidery?" and "Would you be able to cook whatever game I bring home after a long day's hunt?" Her father found it all terribly depressing.

As for the princess, she was quite agreeable to the idea of marriage, as long as her husband was willing—and meek. In the meantime, the princess spent her time riding about the countryside on her snow-white charger, vanquishing ogres and decapitating seven-headed dragons.

One day, as she was finishing off a nine-header (for a little variety), the Valiant Princess spied a figure leaning out the window of a Very-High-Tower-Without-Any-Way-Out that a dragon had been guarding.

"I say," shouted the figure, in a decidedly masculine voice. "I say, are you a *princess*?"

"I was the last time I checked!" the princess shouted back. "The question is, are you a *prince*? And if so, what are you doing up there?"

He blushed, and cleared his throat. "Uh, yes, I'm a prince. My Wicked Uncle locked me up in here, and there aren't any exits. Or entrances, for that matter. And that dreadful dragon!" The prince shuddered graphically. "Thanks awfully for killing it!"

"Hey!" exclaimed the princess, as though something had suddenly occurred to her. "Are you as meek as you are timid?"

"I am *not* timid!" he responded indignantly.

"Then tell me what other kind of a prince gets shut up in a tower by his uncle, is scared by a silly nine-headed dragon, and needs someone, namely a princess, to come and rescue him."

"All right, all right. Point made—you don't have to rub it in! Listen, do you know how I could get down from here? As I said, there are no doors, and I don't really fancy the jump."

"Umm, well, I don't know. Let me see if I've got any rope with me . . ."

"Don't you have fantastically long hair that I can climb down on, or something?"

"Good Lord, no. Do you? No, long hair gets in the way all the time. I had mine cut long ago . . . Well, I don't seem to have any rope . . . um . . . wait a minute— I've got it!" Dismounting, the princess shouted, "I'll be back in a minute!"

Several minutes later she reappeared, dragging along the dead dragon by the tail.

"There!" she cried triumphantly, pulling it over to the base of the tower, below the window. "Just jump on that. Dragon tummies are very soft."

Feeling extremely foolish, and hoping desperately that no one could see him, the Timid Prince jumped. In fact, the dragon's tummy was so soft that they spent the next half hour taking turns bouncing up and down on it.

"Say," said the princess, after some of the novelty had worn off. "That's nice embroidery on your shirt. Who did it?"

"Uhh, I did," the prince admitted shamefacedly.

"But only becau—"

"You're *perfect*!" the princess exclaimed happily. "You're meek, you're timid, and you even do embroidery! Will you marry me?"

"What do you mea—"

"I mean I want you to marry me because you're meek and timid and you do embroidery. Nothing could be simpler! Will you?"

"But you're—"

"I'm strong, valiant, and I like to kill dragons!"

"But princes—"

"I know, I know. Princes aren't usually meek and timid. So what? Princes aren't usually locked up in towers and guarded by dragons, either. Why be usual?"

"But what would people thi—"

"Who cares? Look, tell me this. Do you really want to spend your time killing dragons?"

"Well, no . . . not really, but—"

"And do I look as though I want to devote my life to needlework?"

"Uh, no, I guess not, but—"

"So what's your problem? Come on! Let's go home and tell Daddy."

The prince sighed. "OK, but on one condition."

"What?"

"That you occasionally let me say something."

"Deal!" exclaimed the princess. And off they went.

Soon after, they were married and settled into the castle that was the princess's father's wedding present. It was situated at the edge of a large magical forest where the princess could hunt and the prince could bird-watch. And there they lived happily, if unusually, until they died.

ABOUT THE AUTHOR

Heather Garrett lives in Urbana, Illinois, where she is a student at University High School. She enjoys writing stories for people she knows; "The Valiant Princess" was written for her cousin.

Would he ever stop searching for his mother?

Without the Imagination

by HENRY CLARKE

O rphaned at birth, I'd grown up in the Missoula Home for Boys. I was born there, but never left with my mother. I doubt she ever saw me. I was never breast-fed; they say I accepted a bottle on the first try. I didn't even have the instincts of a regular boy.

We were not allowed to watch television at the Home (*Home* always emphasized by the attendants), and I'm glad. The typical television family might have overwhelmed me. I couldn't have watched Dennis Mitchell play with Mr. Wilson in suburbia while I sat unwanted, wedged in the armpit of Montana.

So my years at the Home were spent squirming in school (I completed grade twelve) and tending the small animals kept out behind the central building. I loved the dogs and goats and sheep that lolled in the back. The parents of the newborns would protect them from the wild animals and from foul weather, and, once I became familiar to the animals, they would protect me also. After dark, I'd sit on the ground, patting the dogs, and they would gather around and lie near me. Once, when we heard a coyote, they all got up and circled me, their hackles raised in my defense.

When I finally left the Home at eighteen (I was the oldest resident in the Home's history), they gave me Lady, my favorite black Lab. I'd trained her from her birth when I was thirteen; she was my best friend. The people at the Home said she had very fancy parents, but the owners couldn't cope with all the puppies, so they gave one to the Home. When they gave me her pedigree (not the kind of thing often found at an orphanage), I read her full name: Repentant Lady. I threw out the slip of paper and renamed her Mary.

I drove through Montana, making money wherever I could. I cut grass in Brockway, scrubbed dishes in Vandalia, and sold TVs at a Radio Shack in Polson on the edge of Flathead Lake. As I drove from job to job, Mary would lie quietly on the seat of my truck, and I'd rub her soft ears as I drove. My independence made me feel adult and mature. It also made me think of what it would be like to have a family, of how wonderful it would be to be driving home for Christmas.

Sometimes I'd see myself in the mirrors as I looked around at Montana, and I'd fantasize about what my mother looked like. I was sure she was pretty, but not beautiful. I didn't have the dainty features that a beautiful mother dictates in her offspring. She was probably of average height, since I was just under six feet. I also knew she would be young, because orphans are usually left by young mothers. I'd look at every woman I saw and compare them to myself, hoping someday to find a match.

I liked to think of my mother as a glamorous woman, but I did not see her in Great Falls or at a ski resort. I thought I saw her once, in a town later identified to me as "the one between Cohagen and Jordan." I had a road atlas, but there was no marked town along that stretch of Montana.

The ability of the human to live on hope is incredible. Long, cold, rainy nights were made palatable by the thought of my mother. As a grade-school student can get through math class by thinking about stickball at recess, so could I get through huge spells of loneliness by imagining my mother; she, too, must have been searching.

Mary was sitting on the seat beside me when I pulled into the small diner along the side of Route 59. She was pregnant, due any day. I'd bred her to a stud in Great Falls; I needed the money her pups would bring. I'd never had a family, so I wondered what I'd do when Mary's family appeared. Her stomach bulged under her, seeming to sweep the ground, and when she ran, her overflowing teats flapped and slapped against each other like a screen door against its frame. In the latter part of her pregnancy, Mary had become very protective of me; she wouldn't let strangers advance on me without barking and raising the fur on the back of her neck. She worried, too. She'd walk tiny circles on the seat of the truck, sniffing and exploring the same two feet of synthetic leather again and again; then she'd flop wearily down in the middle of her circle. I would just look over at her and wait for the puppies to arrive, right there in the Ford. She would lie very close to me and put her head in my lap.

The diner was disheveled. An overflowing Dumpster squatted off to one side, and a decrepit row of
cabins stood behind the restaurant. The curtains were
orange and brown, dusty and ripped, and the cover-
ings on the booths and counter stools inside were vinyl;
bits of stuffing jutted out from the seats.

I usually looked for my mother in public places—
movie theaters or restaurants. Some people showed
traits that I exhibited—the same jawbone, the same
rhythm of breathing—but never more than one or two
parts of me would match anyone else. I knew that
someday I'd find my mother, and she would just know
me, and we'd love each other and take care of each
other.

I entered the diner through the ripped screen door,
sat down at the counter, and ordered a cup of coffee
and a huckleberry muffin. The lady running the place
was grotesque: huge bags hanging below her eyes and
girdled blobs of fat pushing out around her cinched
apron. Canadian bacon popped on the long griddle
behind her, coating the splatter-guard with grease and
warm fat. A 45 spun in an old jukebox that was pushed
back into the corner, its lights flickering as the bulbs
wore down. The coffee was good, but the muffin was
stale. It was dried out, and the berries were dispersed
in a thoughtless pattern. I filled Mary's water dish from
a sink in the grungy little bathroom of the diner and
plodded out to the dirt parking area in front.

As I settled the water container in the dust, a little
red Jeep swerved into the lot, throwing dust over its
outside wheels. A tall woman stepped out, her cow-
boy boots settling in the dirt. She was in fashionable
dress: her gripping jeans tucked into the boots, and a

denim shirt tied at the bottom, exposing her navel. Her flat chest and straight hips were hardly feminine, but her face was attractive, blue eyes like my own dominating her other features. I guessed she was about thirty-five. She looked more wealthy than anyone else in that part of Montana. The Jeep was clean and in good condition. She dressed in the current style.

I followed her back into the diner. Her features were similar to my own, and I imagined that her picture in my fictional living room would not look out of place.

She sat at the counter but ordered nothing. The fat woman passed her a "Good morning" and set a cup of black coffee beside her. Her hips expanded over the small round stool as she rolled to one side to reach the cup. She picked her boots up from the footrest under the counter and crossed her legs. She sat elegantly, but her dusty face defeated her clothes in their attempt at an image that was greater than she could support. She wasn't royalty, but she held herself as if she were. Her chin paralleled the counter, pointing her eyes at the wall over the skillet. Her ears twitched a little when she blinked.

Her body fit the picture of my mother that I had constructed over my lifetime. Her features were very similar to mine, and any father could make up for the differences. I stared at her for a long time. She sat as I did, and when she spoke to the cook, her sweet voice had the same tone as mine.

She could have raised me in a little ranch house, riding horses and living together for years. She could have loved me all my life, never regretting her decision to keep me. Instead, I had been discarded at birth.

But that could be forgiven. I could forget all that and take her now with any past we chose. She was a perfect match. All her features matched my own—her hair, her cheeks, her eyes.

It is amazing that I was still letting my mind race into fantasies of a family and of a mother. After almost twenty years of being an orphan, I should have hardened myself against the hope of ever finding her. I knew she would never simply announce herself at the Missoula Home for Boys and whisk me away. I knew as well as I knew my times tables that she would not drive up and take me to a farm and raise me in the Corn Belt. But a human body does not allow its user to abandon hope. Hope fuels the body, a hope that better times and a better life are on the way, maybe just a day away.

I knew this woman was my mother after a few moments of studying her, but then she did something that convinced me so much I was ready to introduce myself.

My mother looked deliberately at me and said, flat in tone, with no emotion, "It's so nice that the sun's out today."

I said nothing. I could say nothing. She knew I was her son. I had found my mother after agonizing years of hope and grievance. She wanted me back. She hadn't wanted to give me up—she'd been forced to—and wonderful fate had brought us to the same point on this day of our separate quests.

A Volkswagen sputtered into the lot, and my mother looked away from me and stood up stiffly. She walked past me to the door. She greeted the man who got out of the car with a kiss on the cheek. He was disgusting; his skin was pale and rutty, and his business suit was grimy and of an unpleasant cut. He was very thin, and his thick beard made his head appear too heavy for the rest of him. His inflated head made me wonder if he ever had to prop it up to keep it from tumbling off and rolling down his horrid suit.

The two walked to one of the dilapidated cabins behind the diner and quickly went in. I followed and stopped just around the corner. They drew the blinds hurriedly and locked the door. I watched intently for half an hour, then saw them come back out. The man had forgotten to put his tie back on, and the woman's hair hung down out of its style. Her shirt was untied and not buttoned far enough up. He gave her a wad of bills and walked to the front of the diner. He opened the door to his shabby compact and plopped in. The car popped away down Route 59.

She entered the back of the diner through a small plywood door and tiny hall that led her behind the counter. I looked into the building through the ripped curtains and saw my mother give some of the bills to the old woman behind the counter. They laughed as my mother tied her hair back out of her face.

I stared at the small cabin where my mother had offended me so many times. I was starting for the truck when I heard Mary yelp from somewhere in the bushes. She had been loose in the lot since my mother drove up, and had wandered off behind the Dumpster. I called to her, but she only barked back from the same place. I crashed into the bushes and found her beneath a berry bush, kindly licking clean her pups. There were four, all black. Their fur was slicked back like a teenager's in the fifties, their eyes closed like frightened children's

in a spookhouse. Mary stood up to greet me and re-
vealed one dead pup, crushed by the weight of its mother.

I gathered up the living puppies and put the dead
one in the Dumpster. I thought that Mary might get
upset, so I let her watch me, but she didn't care about
the dead one; it was no longer her responsibility. I put
them in my coat on the seat of the truck. Mary wad-
dled into the truck, the pain and effort of delivery still
with her. She licked them all again, and then allowed
them to feed from her abundant supply of breast milk.

Pulling out of the diner, I let my mind go blank. I
stared at the white line on the side of the road, not
seeing anything of Montana as it rushed by me. I put
a horse blanket over Mary and her pups and tried desperately to keep them within its warmth, but they always squirmed their way out.

Every time I saw myself in the mirror I became en-
raged. I'd pound on the wheel of the truck, scaring
Mary and her puppies. Sometimes I would thrash myself into tears, then collapse, drooping over the wheel
and cursing my taunting reflection as it looked at me
from the windshield. I could see my mother everywhere.

I ran deeper into the state, my eyes fixed on the
broken white line, my gas gauge slowly winding down.
I ran out of gas climbing a huge deserted mountain,
my foot heavy on the accelerator. I gripped the wheel
of the truck for a long time, just staring at the white
line and concentrating on the road ahead of me. Hoping
that the truck would have a sudden surge of power
and travel on its own, or that I would be rescued . . .

As the sun began its descent behind the mountain,
I eased out of my position in the cockpit and put my

back against the seat. My fingers were cramped from hours of strangling the steering wheel, and my right leg was tingly numb. Lying down on the seat, I put my head on the edge of the blanket, curled up against Mary and her sleeping babies, and sobbed.

ABOUT THE AUTHOR

Henry Clarke attends Phillips Exeter Academy in Exeter, New Hampshire; his hometown is Dobbs Ferry, New York. An honor student, he plays ice hockey and is catcher for his school's varsity baseball team. A DJ at Exeter's radio station, WPEA, he has also served as the yearbook sports editor for three years and has twice won his school's English Prize.

Story Index
By genre, topic, and for use as writing models